Mick

By

Willie Orr

TP

ThunderPoint Publishing Ltd.

First Published in Great Britain in 2019 by
ThunderPoint Publishing Limited
Summit House
4-5 Mitchell Street
Edinburgh
Scotland EH6 7BD

Cover Images © Homer Sykes / Alamy Stock Photo
Cover Design © Huw Francis

ISBN: 978-1-910946-61-9 (Paperback)
ISBN: 978-1-910946-62-6 (eBook)

www.thunderpoint.scot

Acknowledgements

First I would like to acknowledge the excellent work of Lynn Abrams in her publication *The Orphan Country*. Edinburgh. 1998. Shining a spotlight in the darkness of 'boarded-out' children and the thousands of young people placed in 'care' in Scotland, it proved to be an invaluable resource. Through her research I was able to locate primary sources which provided authentic background material. My thanks to the staff of the Mitchell Library, Glasgow, for their help in giving me access to these sources. I would also like to thank the many 'boarded-out' boys whom I met while I worked in the West Highlands and Islands and who shared with me their experiences – good and bad. Many thanks too to Seonaid Francis for her help in editing the MS and for risking publication. Most of all, my thanks to Jan, my wife, who not only endures my absences – physical and mental – with supreme patience but also acts as my best critic, proof-reader and irreplaceable friend.

Dedication

To Jan
IOE.

Chapter 1
MICK

O God, he's back.

There's his nailed boots on the back step an the clink of the milk pail on the door. He'll go through to the pantry an tip the milk into the cooler an swirl the pail under the cold tap an then he'll be through here. Jesus God. Those hands. Fingers like cow teats but cracked an calloused an stronger than a vice. Can lift a sack of corn with one hand an prise my mouth open without strainin. O God help me. He's kickin the mud off his boots at the door. I'll have to get out but it's too sore, the twine round ma wrists. Can't pull it. Can't stand the pain. Skin's rubbed through tryin to work loose from the lavvy seat. One time I was tied to a chair through there an shat myself when he squeezed ma lips with pliers.

'Breathe through your nose, you wee bastard,' he shouted, 'How many times have I told you. You look so glaikit with your mouth hangin open.'

Wish I could run, run out of the yard, through the trees. What's the use, though? Just be caught again an whipped with that 'lectric cable.

Jesus, there he's in the pantry. He'll be here in a minute. God help me. Please, please, please, take me away. Mustn't show I'm afraid, though. Grip ma teeth together an stare at the floor. He goes in a right rage when you show you're afraid or if you plead with him. When he slaps your face it's like a hot iron on your skull, like you were branded like a beast.

An she's worse. Tied to ma chair in the kitchen, she cuddled me into her chest.

'Poor wee bairn,' she said. 'Poor wee bairn's no mammy nor daddy.'

Can smell her sweat and fag smoke and clothes not washed while he pulled my head back by the hair an spooned cauld porridge down ma throat.

'Poor wee bairn. Mammy's a whore and daddy's a drunk. Poor

wee bairn.'

Times she tries to be nice too. Smiles an leaves a chocolate in front of me an then he says I stole it.

Wish I could drown her. Fling her in the sheep dip an keep her head under till the bubbles stop.

There's the pail washed. Any minute now.

***

'I'll have to take my wellingtons today. I'm going to visit the Munros' farm. Unannounced.'

George Buchanan, Childrens' Officer, winds his watch and slips it into his waistcoat pocket. His wife clears the breakfast table behind him as he folds his napkin neatly and lays it on the table.

'A surprise visit ? They might not be there.'

'I don't think they leave the place very often.'

'The back of beyond.'

'Yes. A bit remote. I'm not altogether happy about the placement of the boy. There's something about the couple. A bit too keen to please, obsequious, as if they are hiding something. Still, they promised to look after him so I gave them the benefit of the doubt. I hope I was not mistaken again.'

'I don't know how they scratch a living out of that place.'

'Poor, sour land right enough, covered in rashes. Milk cows skeletally thin, flanks caked with dung. A bad sign. Yet the pigs seem to thrive. Now that's a puzzle, my dear, a puzzle.'

'Probably likes bacon. You'll be back for dinner?'

'As long as I don't meet a catastrophe and have to remove the boy.'

He brushes the crumbs from his tweed trousers, pats his pocket to ensure that his pipe and tobacco have been remembered and goes through to the hall. He examines his reflection in the mirror of the hall-stand and smooths down a stray lock of silver hair, hauls on his ex-army waterproof coat and picks up his wellingtons.

'Bye, dear. Back for dinner.'

A tall man, he stoops as he passes under the lintel.

***

Ma pal ran away. Not from here like, from the orphanage. They found him frosted to the leaves in a wood. Musta got lost. He was runnin home to his Ma in the city.

The cleek on the door clicks an he stands over me. There's cow-dung on his boots an a splash o milk. Don't look up. Guts are dropping into ma arse and ma heart is jumpin about like mad. Grip ma fists tight, waitin for the blow.

'Where's Betsy ?' he says.

I shake ma head.

'Stupid wee bastard. You never know anything.'

An he leaves. God answered me. Stop shakin for Christ sake. It's hard to relax, though, when you're bent double with your hands and legs tied to the seat. At least I can pee without it spillin over the chair. Last time I was tied in the kitchen he left me in ma own pee an shit till it burnt ma skin. She made him let me off 'cos she couldn't stand the smell.

How could he not see, the inspector, see what they're like? They put on a great show. All smiles an 'sir'. Wash the cups an make scones an wash theirselves. Bastards. You want to tell him, it's fair burstin out of you but you hold it in.

'One fucken word out of you and I'll whip the skin off your back.'

He would too. Even when the inspector talks to you outside you say nothin. We all know that. Don't say a word. Cause trouble and it's all your fault. Can't trust any of them.

Inspector has kind eyes an quiet voice an smellsa pipe smoke but tell him an they'll deny it all an flog you after till you pass out. You're in a pit with a pack of wolves, boy. Tongues out over the fangs, slaverin, round an round, watchin you, waitin for the right time. Now an again one races at you, snaps at your leg, tears at the skin an runs away. One day it'll be your throat.

Davey escaped. No fear, Davey. Used to steal food in the home for the rest of us. Always gettin the strap for that an for speaking back an for not learnin the psalms. Had his head shaved for ringworm but there was no ringworm there. They knew that fine. If you pee'd the bed you had to wash your own sheets with a sign on your back an they made Davey wash his when they were dry.

3

One night after tea they loaded some of the boys into a car an drove round the country tryin to get folk to take them in. Davey was the last to go. Farm folk could see the anger in him, the way he looked sideways at you with slit eyes like a bad dog.

'Betsy,' Munro shouts, 'where the hell are you?'

Christ he's in a bad temper.

'Am in the calf house, you dope. Mucking them out. I told you.'

'Go in there and louse that boy and get him to do it.'

Relax. Means he's not comin.

'Louse him yourself you lazy bastard.'

God, is he comin after all?

'I'm taking the cows out to the stubble.'

'Excuses, excuses. I'll do it after.'

Ma arse is sore, tied in the same place.

Davey like a bad dog. He had that look. The folk he went to weren't much better than these. Said he was lazy. Hauled him on a pulley in the barn and let the rope go. Knocked all the breath outa him. They sent him back to the home. He grinned as he came in the door.

Some poor souls in there. Mind one bangin his head on the wall at night till he fell asleep, thud, thud, thud. You prayed for it to stop. Another sucked his thumb even after they smeared it with mustard and dipped it in carbolic. He never spoke that one.

'Christ, Betsy!' he shouts, 'It's the Officer! His car at the road end. Get that kid loused and dressed. Fuck's sake, Betsy. He never said he was coming. Hurry for God's sake.

Louse the kid!'

She barges in with a knife in her hand. Going to cut ma throat. Jump back an yell but no, she's gonna cut the twine. Christ the twine cuts into ma skin. Knife's blunt.

'It's all right. I'm just cutting you loose.'

Her fingers tremble in the rush. I can see down her front as she bends. Two big udders, wrinkled and white.

'Now get up the stair and put on clean clothes. Hurry up for God's sake and don't come down till you're called.'

Legs are all wobbly tryin to climb the stair. Wood of the steps is warm after the cold floor. Can hardly breathe when I reach the loft. No strength left. Sit on the mattress for a minute. Loft's a safe place usually cos they don't come up here. You can hear everythin going on below through the bare boards, what they say about you and what they're goin to say to the Inspector.

They'll call me down in a minute to speak to him. Maybe I'll tell him the truth, just what they're like, and he'll take me away in the car. Maybe he'd believe me. He took me away from the last place but then the man was dyin of a chest thing. Wife cried when the inspector took me away but he could see for himself it was hopeless. Maybe he'll see this time, see through the lies an wheedlin. But don't be so stupid. It won't happen. Don't get that feelin o hope in your chest. That's the worst thing of all, that wee chink in the dark. When it comes in the night, you clench it tight by the neck like you would kill a chicken so it doesn't get going. You stamp it out before they do.

I hear them muttering downstairs, offerin the man tea.

'I want to see Mick on his own today,' he says. 'Just part of the routine. Is he in the house?'

'He's upstairs. I'll get him down.'

'No, no. I'll go up.'

Christ, he's comin up. Why's he doin that? Better stand in case he thinks I was lyin like a lazy bastard on ma bed. You can tell he's not used to ladders.

'Hello Mick.'

He kneels on the floor cos there's nothin to help him up the last bit. He looks as though he's going to play grizzly bears or somethin on his hands an knees.

'Don't be afraid, Mick. I just wanted to speak to you.'

He struggles to his feet an dusts off his hands. He has to bend cos his head's in the rafters.

'How are you ?'

'All right, sir.'

How can I say anythin else with them listenin down there? Could I whisper it? If I signed to him that I wanted to whisper, would he know what I meant?

'You're very thin. Are you getting enough to eat?'

'Yes, sir.'

'Come over here a minute, son.'

He feels ma ribs.

'A bit too skinny. What are those marks on your wrists? Let me see. How did you get these, Mick? '

Christ, what do I say? I could tell him. The thing inside me wants to tell him. It's blowin up like a bladder ready to burst. Tell him for God's sake. But he won't believe me. I know he won't an they're downstairs waitin.

'I was swingin on a tree, sir. On a rope like Tarzan. I was playin a game.'

'Indeed? Lift up your simmet.'

He looks at the bruises.

'And I suppose these were from the game too.'

'I fell, sir'

'Are you happy here, Mick?'

'Yes, sir.'

'You can tell me in confidence if you're not. You can trust me.'

'Yes, sir.'

'Good lad. Keep it up. You're doing well.'

He pats me on the shoulder and turns to go down the ladder but he swithers at the top. He doesn't know how to go down. In the end he goes down on his knees again and backs away, trying to find the steps with his foot. He looks so stupid I want to laugh.

I can hear them downstairs.

'Mick is far too thin, Mrs Munro. You must see that he eats properly. You are well enough paid to see to that.'

'I can assure you that he gets plenty of meat, sir. The same as ourselves. Whatever we have, he has and sometimes we go without to make sure he has enough. Don't you worry about that, sir.'

'How is he doing, Mr Munro? Is his work satisfactory?'

'Doing very well, sir. A bit of a slacker if he's not watched, but they're all like that nowadays, aren't they? Turn your back and they're half asleep. Mick's a good boy on the whole.'

'And these fearful marks on his wrists. How were they obtained?'

'He was swinging on a rope hanging from a tree, playing like any healthy youngster.'

They were listenin. I knew they were. Just as well I didn't say.

'They are not made by a rope. Something finer, I think.'

'We whiles make rope from baler twine.'

'I suppose it could be that. See that the wounds do not

suppurate.'

'I'll treat them with some sulphur and archangel tar.'

'Is that all you have?'

'We use it for cuts on the sheep and it does fine for that.'

'I'll take your word for it. I'll be back in a month to see how he is.'

'Will you not stay for a cup of tea, sir?'

'Thank you, no. I have other places to visit. Good day to you.'

***

George fills his pipe, carefully tamps down the tobacco and lights it with a match. Puffs of smoke pop from the corner of his mouth.

'I'm not at all happy about that boy.'

He frowns as he gazes into the coal fire.

'I can see that. You never said a word through dinner.'

His wife was deftly darning one of his socks, the wool stretched over a wooden mushroom.

'Sorry. I was preoccupied.'

'You were. What worries you particularly?'

'He has these rope marks on his wrists – wounds really. The boy claims that he received them while playing Tarzan and the couple confirm his story.'

'Nonsense. All carefully rehearsed.'

'Yes. I think I agree. Another surprise visit is in order. The Munros were clearly flustered by the visit today.'

'Maybe when he goes back to school he'll talk to someone.'

'I don't think so. He never says a word. Doesn't trust any of us. Pity about the last farm. They were good people but she had no choice really. She just couldn't manage the place.'

'It sounds as though it's not going to work.'

'Back to a home then. I don't want that.'

Chapter 2
MICK

'What did you say to that man?'

'Nothing. I swear to God. Nothing.'

'Aye well. If I find out you did, I'll thrash the livin daylights outa you.'

He believes me. At least I think he does. Don't know about her, though. She's lookin at me with narrow eyes.

'Get up there and change outa they clothes and muck out the pigs.'

I hurry up the ladder before she says somethin.

I like the pigs, although they stink. Their wee beady eyes watchin you as you muck out the pen an the snouts that make that snufflin noise. You get used to the smell but it clings to your clothes like it was alive, like it was another skin. If I ran from here, they would find me by the smell.

As I race past him in the kitchen he aims a slap to ma head but I dodge it, step into ma wellies at the door an run out to the midden. The barrow, caked with dung, is heavy an hard to handle but I wheel it round to the pig shed an stop at the pens. You have to watch that they don't get out as you open their gate. You chase them to the back of the pen before you take the barrow in. I let them out once and he jumped up and down with rage. It was a laugh watchin him chase them round the yard but I paid for it later.

The big, wide shovel is all right for him but for me it's hard to keep straight. I spill a lot of the pig shite as I scrape the pen. When I'm done, I wheel the barrow out to the midden. Now comes the hard bit. The midden is big an has three planks one after the other. You have to race the barrow up the first plank an keep your balance. If the wheel misses the plank, it sinks into the shite an, if you lose your balance, you're in it up to your knees. I get ready an take a deepbreath. The planks are greasy an look steepern ever. I grip the barrow handles an race at the midden. This time it works an I tip the shite into the end of the midden.

Fair pleased with myself I take a breather an look up the lane to the road. If I was going to run, I wouldn't go that way. That's the way they would think I would go. No. Back that way to the trees where the crows nest. But then where? You'd have to keep the road in sight. That's the way to the city. Find my Mam. Don't know where she lives but she's in there somewhere. I'll find her. Don't you worry. An they wouldn't find me, not in there.

I know how to dodge the polis an the sanny woman.

'What are you standin there for, you lazy wee bastard ?'

I jump with fright an drop the barrow in the shite.

'No bloody use for anything. Get down here and cut swedes for the stirks. Hurry up for Christ's sake.'

I tug the barrow out of the midden an head for the turnip shed.

One day I will run. I will. Over to the trees. When, though? Better at night but I can't get down from the loft without wakin them an they're watchin me all day. They did go to a sale once an left me here but they tied me to the lavvy seat an locked the door. But there will be a time. Just have to wait.

I lift the spade an slice some turnips into bits an put them in a wire basket an then heave them into the turnip cutter. Takes strength to turn the handle but I can just manage it. Funny smell, sliced neeps, like pepper, as they fall into the basket. I carry them round an feed them into one of the troughs in the byre. The stirks love them.

Maybe when the school starts. That would be a chance. Would be like the thing if she took me every day, though, an got me at night. She couldn't but. Not every day. Just one day that's all I need. Back to my Mam. Beautiful, my Mam, always laughing. Bloody sanny lady.

***

George flicks through the file, wondering what to write under Subsequent History of the Case. He frowns as he reads the first comments of Simpson, another Officer, all carefully typed. Why could the man not write like everyone else? One of these young whippersnappers keen to display his skills. His own hand had been perfected when he had to practise between ruled lines in the book. His was clear, precise, elegant.

He glanced through the history.

'Children utterly neglected by mother, improperly fed, clothed and tended.

Mother living in one of the lowest lodging houses in the city and her two children painfully exposed to all kinds of vice and immorality. A hawker and woman of bad character.'

Both the children had been taken into care and their mother forced to sign an agreement allowing the Committee to send them anywhere in the world. He did not approve of that. The condition seemed unnecessarily harsh. He had seen mothers who, under the most intolerable circumstances, had tried to keep the family together. He remembered Maggie Ewart whose man had been killed when his jacket caught in an industrial lathe and he was smashed like a doll against the machine. She had worked from before dawn till after dusk scrubbing floors, taking in washing, cleaning for big houses, anything to earn a pittance, but she had worn herself out and, in spite of her protests, the children were taken away anyway. Perhaps Mick's mother was like that. Perhaps she had tried too. Some members of the Committee had no idea what women in the city slums had to suffer and the strength they needed to survive.

He reads what he had written after his first visit to Mick's last placement:

'Boy very happy. Couple pleased to have him. Say that he works well on the farm and helps in the house. Boy says that he is happy in school. Wants to know where his sister is living.'

Sad. The farmer had contracted lung cancer and his wife had to relinquish the tenancy. The placement had been so promising – unlike the Munros.

He wants to set down his suspicions but he needs some hard evidence before he can commit them to paper.

He lifts his fountain pen and smooths down the file.

'Mick is worryingly thin and has wounds on his wrists which he claims he received in play. Foster parents confirm this. They say that his work is satisfactory but needs watching. They complain that 25 shillings does not cover expenses.'

He signs the document, lays down his pen and sits back, remembering Mick cowering in the corner of the loft as he climbed the ladder.

A poor farm, the Munros'. The lane leading up to the steadings was almost impassable with deep twin ruts worn by the tractor and brambles hanging from the steep banks. The farm house showing all the signs of returning to nature, its gutters growing weeds, its slates green with lichen, its gable and chimney smothered under a heap of ivy. The shaws of the potato crop struggling to pierce a blanket of weeds and foggage in the hay field sprouting clumps of rashes above the choked drains. Slack fences hung with wool like washing lines where sheep had barged their way through. The midden leaking foul-smelling liquid across the yard.

On his first visit he had been on the point of turning back as a snarling collie, its teeth bared, sprang at his hand every time he reached to undo the gate hasp. Munro, however, had appeared, roared at the dog which slunk away, and came down to meet him. A sturdy man with a permanent frown and eyes which were never still, flitting from one thing to another as if an enemy might leap out from any direction, he had greeted him with a crunching handshake. His massive hand swallowed his own and the muscle on his arm rippled like a serpent. The fabric over the peak of his tweed cap was worn away, his collarless shirt damp with sweat and his bib and brace overalls glistened with grease. The first impression had been one of an honest, hard-working farmer. It was the way he and his wife glanced at each other in the kitchen before they spoke that caused concern. The room had been cleaned and scrubbed for his arrival, the concrete floor still wet and the hearth gleaming. The wife had actually curtsied as he reached to shake her hand and, unlike her husband, had looked him in the eye and smiled. Yet there was something untrustworthy about her, something he could not fathom, and he was known to be a good judge of character.

He had asked to see the boy's bedroom and she explained that they only had the loft above the kitchen, they themselves sleeping downstairs in the next room. The loft had been swept and a hair mattress placed on the floor. The eiderdown and blankets, she said, were on their way. There was no electric light in the loft but she promised a Tilley lamp and a torch, the toilet being downstairs. The accommodation was far from satisfactory but the Committee was so short of foster placements that he had to take the risk.

George rises from his desk and gazes out across the back garden. His roses are spectacular, blazing in the evening sun. The Compassion on the fence is magnificent. He inhales, imagining its sweet scent. Beyond the roses the potatoes are in bloom in the vegetable patch, their blue flowers shimmering in the breeze. Edzell blues, his favourite. He compares their abundance to Munro's poor specimens and wonders why Munro can't find the time to weed his crop.

He and his wife had no children. In some ways he regretted that but, when he saw the misery and suffering which many orphan children had to endure, the shadow of his progeny possibly assigned to that fate frightened him. Many respectable parents through accident, illness or disablement had been reduced to penury and their children removed. He could not bear the thought of his children ending up in a home. In one home menstruating girls had to have baths in disinfectant and were not supplied with sanitary towels. In another boys were punished with the strap for failing to learn a psalm. His memory was often disturbed by images of children sitting rocking on their beds, their eyes fixed blankly on the floor and their thumbs in their mouths. Still, he knew there were successes. One of his boys placed on a croft had just graduated from university, another had gained a Master's certificate at sea. He wondered whether the boys had been born with that ability, whether the parents, failing perhaps through no fault of their own, had passed on intelligence or whether the successes had been due to foster parents chosen by him. Or was it all a matter of luck? Probably. All a bit of a lottery. He sighed and walked through to the living room.

'I'm just going to polish my shoes.'

'Well see and put down some newspaper.'

He frowned at his wife and walked through to the kitchen, opened the cupboard, laid a sheet of newspaper on the floor and reached for his shoe-cleaning box. Everything laid our neatly – tin of polish, application cloth, duster. Shoes to be cleaned carefully on the paper. One thing he had learnt in the army was the technique of shining his shoes so that he could see his face in the polish. He filled the polish lid with a little water and sat down, dipped the cloth first in the water and then in the polish and started to apply the black wax in tiny circles on the toe of a shoe. He had had a comfortable war. Sometimes he felt guilty about that, having spent those years in the safety of an English manor house as a wireless instructor, a vital contribution of course but not as dangerous an occupation as that of the agents he trained for France. Most of them, he understood, never returned.

He could still read and send Morse and often talked to himself by tapping out messages. 'Pianists' they were called, the wireless operators. With his left hand he tapped out a signal M U N R O I S   A   B U L L Y.

Chapter 3
MICK

I hate school. The way they call you names, all they posh kids. They know you're not one o them. Jersey too wee an trousers too long hangin down ablow your knee. An it's a new school an that's worse. Teachers don't like you. You get the strap for nothin, like wipin your snot on your sleeve or gettin your tables wrong. It's the only chance, though, to get back to ma Mam. Bet they'll take me to school. Never let me go on ma own.

Today was potatoes. Sent out with a graip an a wire basket and a sack.

'One graip mark and I'll mark your arse.'

How can you dig tatties without stickin the fork in one of them? You can't even see them under the ground.

'The Epicures, mind. Don't look so glaikit. I showed you.'

I went up to the field an looked at the drills. Were all the same an I couldn't remember what he said. I was so scared I would get it wrong but then I saw one shaw had been dug an I stuck the graip in the next one well behind the shaw an shook out the tatties. There they were all white an clean an not a fork mark. Clever boy, Mick.

I turned to see if he was watchin. No-one there so I stood an looked at the trees.

If I ran from the school, it would be a different way. Not by the roads. They would catch you that way an I'd get lost across the fields. Then I saw this puff of smoke miles away an I says, the railway, that's the way. Walk the track. That's the way back to Glasgow. Clever boy, Mick. That'll beat the bastards.

What do you eat, though, on the run? Steal eggs. That's risky, goin near the farms. Milk from doorsteps. Okay in the town but not out here. Grab a hen but Jesus you could be hung for that or sent to the gaol or sent to Australia. How do you do it? Can't be Davy Crockett here and hunt animals. Money. You need money. I could nick off of them. I know where she keeps it, the bitch. But how do you buy things? Go into a shop and they'll know you're on the run an call the polis. You need a stash, Mick. Nick wee bitsa things, cheese an bacon an things. Wee bits so they don't see. Stash them away in a hidin place. You've got it, boy...

I brought back the tatties, a whole half bag of them and he timmed them out on the floor to look for fork marks. Not one. The bastard. You could see he wanted to find one.

'Is this all you got?'

'All I could carry.'

'Aye. A right jessie you. Bloody useless. Go and cut firewood till milking.'

I got the bushman saw from the shed an went round to the saw horse. Last time I broke the blade on a staple stuck in an old stob. He went wild at that an slapped me across the face. He cut himself when he fitted the new blade it was that sharp an I was pleased when I saw the blood running down his hand. Served him right.

If ma Da was here he would sort him out. Not big but hard as nails. Could lift me off of ma feet with one hand. I mind his smell. Oil an iron an fags. Used to dress up for the dancin an he smelled different, soap and brylcreme. Shaved with a cutthroat. Used to watch the blade shavin off the soap an whiskers makin wee scratchy noises. When he was dead they shaved him but not as good as he did. Left tufts on his chin. They had a job carryin the coffin up the close an they were pechin like pigs when they got to the door. He lay in the room with his eyes shut an a bandage round the top of his head an where his arm was.

'What did they do with his arm?' I says.

'Shush.' Red John was frownin and lookin over at my Ma.

She was sittin in the chair greetin with her face in her hands.

'Stupid,' Calum from across the stair says to his Da.

Biggern me but I burst his nose outside the cludgie in the back close. Wish I could burst Munro's nose. I didn't greet at the funeral. Not me. Ma wouldn't stop. We hugged her in the bed at night, me and my sister, but she went on and on till I you'd think she'd run outa water. I couldn't stand it an one night I roared at her to shut up. Wish I'd never done that. Ma sister slapped me for it.

I don't know where she is now. They had to lift her away from the close with her heels kicking and her teeth trying to bite their hands and Ma screaming out the window. Never saw her again. We were close, us two. Closern Ma and Da. Used to scratch each other's backs in the bed. It hurt when they took her away, like a knife twirlin in your guts. Never do that again, Mick, get that close to somebody.

'I don't hear that saw, you wee bastard.' Munro is in the byre.

I saw as hard as I can.

'Leave it and go for the cows and see and hang the saw in the shed.'

I do as he says an head down to the gate. Start my stash tonight. Makes me grin just thinking about it.

***

George stops the car at the farm road end and changes into his wellingtons. It is a fine day with a warm breeze that ripples the green oats in the field across the road. A better farm altogether with neat thorn hedges, regimented ranks of baled hay and acres of potatoes with not a weed to be seen. He wonders if Munro would have succeeded had he been blessed with better land. Probably not. He did not seem to be a lazy man yet the farm showed all the signs of neglect and indolence.

The lane leading up to the farm is lined with beech trees which, many years before, had formed a hedge. He stops for a moment to enjoy the peace, listening to the rooks in the distance and the sound of a tractor beyond the steadings. A good day. The war in Korea has ended. That conflict, coming so soon after 1945, had horrified him. More young lives to be wasted in hostile country far from home for a cause that he had described as dubious. Still, it is over and that brings a sense of contentment.

There is no-one about when he reaches the yard. Even the crabbit dog is not to be seen and there is no smoke from the chimney. The pungent smell of pigs, however, pervades the premises and hangs around like another person. He reckons that the tractor must be in the field beyond the potatoes and heads in that direction.

Munro is seated on the Ferguson sweeping hay into piles with a buckrake. His wife and Mick are building a ruck, heaving pitch-forks of hay on to its foundation. They don't see him at first and he stands at the gate watching them. Peasants have been repeating this task for centuries, he thinks, making fodder for their cattle, harvesting their crops to survive the winter. Season after season, struggling to avoid starvation. Not much progress really. A tractor instead of a horse but man still battling with the weather and still slaughtering his own kind. Munro sees him, stops the tractor and walks to meet him.

'Good day, Mr Buchanan.'

'Wonderful day. Perfect for the hay'

'It's dry at any rate. Have to get it up before the rain.'

'You've got good help I see.'

'Aye. He's a good lad. Most of the time anyway.'

'I would like to speak to him, if you don't mind. It won't take long. Soon be time for school and I need to have a chat about that.'

'Fair enough, sir. I'll send him up. I'm sure we can manage without him for a few minutes.'

Munro turns away and hurries back to the ruck. George watches him take the fork from Mick's hands and prod him in the chest with his finger.

Mick ambles up to the gate. George sees that the wounds on his wrists are not healing.

'Well, Mick. You're good with the pitch-fork. Do you enjoy that work?'

'Yes, sir.'

'Walk with me a bit, Mick. I have something for you in the car.'

'I was told to be quick. There's work to be done.'

'Mr Munro will understand. Come.'

Mick walks beside him with his head slightly turned away.

'School soon, Mick. What do you think about that?'

'Good, sir.'

'Quite happy about a new school?'

Mick says nothing.

'Are you worried?'

'They'll call me names.'

'And how will you respond?'

'Do nothing.'

'That's not how you dealt with it last time. You reacted violently and one of the pupils was sent to hospital.'

'I won't. I'll be good.'

'If they call you names, you tell the teacher.'

Mick says nothing. Of course he says nothing. George knows that the teacher will reprimand the offending pupils, making sure that they know that Mick is a tell-tale. The boy will be ostracised and possibly assaulted on the way home. Teachers that sympathise with boarded-out children are thin on the ground.

'Are you happy with the Munros?'

'Yes, sir.'

He stops and places his hand on Mick's shoulder.

'Truly? We are alone here, Mick. You can trust me. If you have complaints, I will not tell the Munros that you have spoken to me but I will find a way of dealing with them. Do you understand?'

'Yes, sir.

'And are you happy with them?'

'I am, aye.'

George sighs and walks on. Why do they never trust him? He does everything he can to ensure that his charges are treated well and many of them are placed with good, God-fearing people. Yet, even when the placement is a success, the children maintain a polite distance, an impenetrable reservation.

When they reach the car he lifts out a brown paper parcel.

'Some school clothes, Mick, and new boots. I think they will fit better than the last lot. See and look after them. I'm sure Mrs Munro will have boot polish. Polish them every day.'

'Thank you, sir.'

'Now away you go back to the hay. I'm sure they'll be missing you. I will call again soon. Goodbye, Mick.'

'Goodbye, sir.'

He watches him shambling up the lane with his parcel under his arm, a small figure under the towering beech trees. Slim beams of sunlight sporadically blaze in the boy's copper hair. He will speak to the teacher before Mick enrols in the school, explain about Mick's background and ask her to look out for any signs of maltreatment. She will, no doubt, agree enthusiastically. Most of them do, wishing to be seen as compassionate people, and many of them have the best of intentions, but few of them will risk antagonising local parents by defending orphan children against peers or foster parents. He doesn't blame the teachers. So many parents in country schools complain about the presence of troubled city children as a bad influence in their schools. Still, he will use all of his charm to win the teacher's sympathy.

Chapter 4
MICK

She held on to ma collar the whole way to school and never spoke. Not like her. Didn't have time to get ma stash. We stop at the gate. Ma socks keep falling down an they'll laugh at that. I'll burst their fucken noses, the wee bastards. She swings me round an shakes my neck.

'Say one wrong word, boy, and I'll flay you alive. She'll tell me, don't you worry. I'll ask the teacher when I come for you.'

I can see them looking at me. They'll have garters in their socks.

The teacher comes out an rings the bell and they go into lines.

'Go on. Hurry up.'

She shoves me at the gate.

My guts are turnin over but I go over an stand in the boys' line. The boys look at me all the way an say nothin. I go to the back. The boy in front of me holds his nose an grins at the other. I want to kick his heel but I've got to be good cos I'm going to do a runner.

We go into the classroom an she calls me over an stands beside me in front of the class. She smells of mothballs.

'Good morning, children.'

'Good morning, Miss Dunlop,' they all say.

'We have a new boy today and I want you all to welcome him to our school. His name is Mick and he is living with Mr and Mrs Munro. I'm sure we can all imagine what it is like to arrive in a new school and how hard it is to make friends so I hope you will all try to make friends with Mick. Now go to your desk Mick – the one just there beside little Craig.'

I go down to the empty desk an put the seat down an sit. The boys beside me are all youngern me. She's put me with the P Ones.

She comes down with a jotter an a pencil. She has shoes like a wee girl an they clatter on the floor.

'Now Mick I want you to write your name inside on the first page while the others say their tables. You can stay in your seat but I like everybody to stand when they say their tables.'

I hate writing. I can't make the pencil do the right thing. It goes over the lines in the jotter, the worst are the capitals. I hold it as tight as I can till ma fingers shake but it makes no difference. I hold ma other arm over the page so that the wee one beside me can't see.

The others stand up an start to say their tables. Take a breather, Mick.

The ink mark on ma desk looks like a strap coming out of the inkwell. Somebody made it a long time ago. I wonder if there is ink left in the inkwell an poke the pencil in the hole. It comes out with a wee black bit at the bottom. I start to draw an M on ma hand.

'Mick,' she shouts an they all go quiet.

'You're supposed to be writing your name. Please concentrate.'

I wipe the pencil on ma trousers an go back to writing an they go back to sayin their tables.

Dinner time'll be the best time to go. No. That'll be too late. Too near lousin time.

But break'll give them time to look for me. No, better be lunch right enough.

At break we get our milk an I pull off the lid an stand against the wall. Then I go out an wait for the big boys. Two of the girls are playin with a ball against the wall an look at me and smile. I let on not to see them. Don't want the boys seeing me being friendly with girls. The other girls are twirlin a rope with one of them in the middle. She's a good jumper and her pigtails flop up and down as she jumps. The boys are playin football near the gate. Buncha jessies. Can't kick a ball for toffee. I'd like to go and show them how but don't want a fight. Just behave till dinner.

One of the girls comes over.

'Hello Mick.'

I wish she'd leave me alone but she has nice blue eyes and a blue cardy so I nod at her.

'Do you live at the Munros ?'

'Aye.'

'Poor you.'

'Oh aye ? Why's that ?'

'Nothing. Nothing. Do you like it there ?'

'Course.'

'They're not your Mum and Dad, though, are they ?'

'What of it ?'

'Doesn't matter.'

She turns away and skips back to the others. Her socks are pure white and her shoes are shinin. Bet she has a Mum an Dad an lives in a posh house. She's nice, though. I'd like to talk to her more on her own.

The teacher comes out an rings the bell an we line up again. I stand at the front an wait to see if any of the boys says anythin. The big one with the hair oil an long trousers stands next to me.

'You're boarded out, eh ? One of them orphans.'

Kick his leg, Mick. Kick the bastard. Then I remember.

We go in an she gets us round the piano for singin. They all know the song so I just stand there like a dummy.

'One man went to mow, went to mow a meadow.'

Her fingers are like hens' claws scratchin at the notes. The big boy looks at me an grins like I'm stupid cos I don't know the song.

After the singin we go back to our desks an she reads a poem. She says it like she means it.

'A chieftain to the Highlands bound

Cries "Boatman do not tarry !'

She almost greets at the end. God's sake it's only a poem.

The van with the dinners comes in the gate an my guts start to churn. Not long now. The man drivin has a fag in his mouth an his cap is tilted back. The dinner lady comes out an he laughs with her an he grabs the big tubs by the handles an carries them in. I hear him put them down in the kitchen an he says,

'Mince an tatties and cabbage, Mrs Dale. Can't do bettern that, eh? Put hairs on your chest.'

'None of that talk, Mr Morris, thank you very much. The children might hear.'

There's a laugh in her voice, though.

He bangs shut the van door an drives out the gate.

The teacher says it's time for dinner.

'Put your jotters and pencils away and line up at the hatch, youngest at the front as usual.'

Don't know if I can eat ma dinner. Mouth's all dry and guts are shakin. The dinner lady rattles up the hatch door an we stand in line. She flups out mince an tatties an neeps on ma plate an semolina an jam for puddin an I take ma tray over to the desk. Have to eat for God's sake, don't know when I'll get it on the run. Wish I'd got ma stash. Tatties dry an stick in ma mouth. Teacher's lookin at me too as if she can guess. I look at my plate. I hate semolina, it makes me boak. What'll I do ? Nudge the wee boy next to me.

'You want ma puddin?'

'Na. I hate that stuff. She makes you eat it, though.'

Jesus. What'll I do? There'll be a row if I don't eat it. Shovel into ma drawers. Na, it'll run down. Swill round the jam. Swallow it, Mick. Only way. Make a fist like you're gonna fight an gob it in. Don't breathe. Gulp like its snot. Go. Well done, Mick. Another. Think of Mam. Do it for her. Beautiful Mam with the black hair. Another. One more an that's it.

Take my tray up to the hatch an out.

Round the back of the bogs an over the wall. Sneak under hedge, jesus the thorns, bare knees black. Run now. Close to the hedge, up the field. Don't look back. Run, Mick, run. Sheep lookin. Stay still, sheep. Don't run. Ewe an lamb in the way. Swerve round like Bobby Johnston. Back on the pitch. Keep goin but legs rubber an chest burnin. Sick comin up. Stop an boak. Semolina an mince. Run again. Dog barkin at the farm there. Hope not at me. Go on, Mick. You can do it, Mam says. I'm comin Ma. Squeeze through fence into trees. Safer here, take a rest.

Big grey trees like elephant's skin, like arms an legs an wee hairy nuts on the ground. Can you eat them, Ma? Na, better not. Head for the railway, Mick. I'm free, Ma. Away from they bastards an their ropes an their whips. No more kickins or rotten meat stuffed in the mouth. No more creepin around shit-scared of him or sick with the smell of her an her stinkin udders. Free like a bird, like a gull over the seas. Go where you want. Wee bird in the trees here somewhere, chirpin in the leaves, but it's awfu quiet. Wouldn't like to be here in the dark .

Through the railway fence an down on to the track. Listen.

Somebody said put your ears to the rail an you can hear a train comin. Rails are all shiny on the top. Walk on the sleepers not on the stones. Easy. Warm here and nice smell off whins like ice cream. God I could go an ice cream, a big cone. Don't think about it, Mick. Make you hungry. What'll you eat tonight, eh? Didn't thinka that ya daft bastard. No shops up here. Where's that ten shillin note? Aye, here it's all crumpled up. No use with no shops.

Listen, is that a train? Where'll I hide ? Kneel on a sleeper, ear to the track. Nothing. Just a buzz in the ear. Have to work out where to hide. Plan like a commando, black face at night, kill with ma bare hands, buph! Lie low in the day. A place to hide, every step of the way. Plan, that's the trick, and keep going today, though. Walk tonight. How? How do you walk in the dark, Mick? Jesus. No street lights or nothin. God. Black as tar. No such thing as bogles, boy. Grow up.

***

'Sorry I'm late, Miss Dunlop. Good of you to wait.'

'I'm so worried, Mr Henderson.'

'I'm sorry you have had this to contend with. When did he disappear?'

'After lunch. I rang the bell and as soon as the pupils lined up we noticed he was missing. I took the pupils to their desks and asked if anyone had seen Mick. George told me that he had seen him going to the boys' toilets so I asked Mrs Cunningham, the dinner lady, to look but there was no sign of him anywhere. I asked the pupils if he had spoken to any of them or if there had been any bullying or name-calling but they seemed be as puzzled as I was.'

'I called at the Munros on my way over. There was no sign of him there. They did not seem surprised.'

'No. Perhaps he had his reasons to leave. Certainly it has nothing to do with the school. Our children were all very welcoming.'

'Of course. Can you think of anywhere he might hide?'

'There are plenty of barns and empty sheds on the farms. He could be anywhere.'

'I will have to inform the constable.'

'You may not have to. Here's Mrs Munro in a hurry.'

In a hurry indeed, flushed and wheezing like a pair of bellows. I can hear her before she reaches the gate. Her wellingtons are caked with mud and her skirt is hanging down disgracefully.

'The wee bastard!' she shrieks.

'Please Mrs Munro, control yourself. Stop and take a breath and please refrain from using foul language. I can see you're upset. Do calm down.'

'Ten fucken shillings.'

'Mrs Munro! Please. It is most offensive in front of Miss Dunlop.'

'Never mind her. He's stolen ten shillings. My egg money. The thievin wee bastard. If I catch him, I'll whip the skin off his arse.'

'I would hope not, Mrs Munro, and I hope you have never done such thing. I will see that you are compensated. Now, perhaps you could calm down and help us to find the boy. Can you think of anywhere he might hide?'

'Back to the city. That's where he'll go. Back to that whore of a mother of his. Look there. And he can stay there for all I care. Never want to see him again nor any more of his kind. Thievin bastards, the whole lot of them. And I want his keep up till today. Cost me a fortune he has.'

'You will be paid, Mrs Munro. Never fear. Now I must find the constable and inform him about Mick and you will need to report the theft. I can mention it to the constable, if you like, but he will need the have a statement from you.'

'No. Never mind. As long as I get compensation.'

She turns and waddles away, a little calmer than when she arrived.

'Thank you, Miss Dunlop. As I said, my apologies for the distress. I'm afraid these children are a bit unpredictable. Most of them have been through terrible times and are fearfully damaged by their experiences but, thanks to our foster parents, some of them recover and become useful and indeed admirable citizens. I had hoped that Mick, who is an intelligent boy, might mature in such a way.'

'I do hope that he is found, Mr Henderson, and that he is

returned to more suitable foster parents.'

'Yes, I think I have misjudged the Munros. Mea Culpa, Miss Dunlop. But we are so short of good placements. However, we will need to find him first. Thank you for your help. Good evening'

Chapter 5
SLIGO

The river Clyde glitters in the sun while, beneath the surface, it drags the city's toxic sludge towards the sea. A raft of debris – battens, boxes, straw and a mattress – swirls under the bridge. Gulls quarrel over a pail of slops flung from a steamer on the Broomielaw. Yesterday's rain lingers in the gutters stained with rainbows of oil. The city's veins pulse sluggishly with trams, buses, trucks and cars. It tries to breathe but its lungs shudder and sigh. The air tastes of sulphur and soot. A hostel for homeless men stands five storeys high, its columned doorway a legacy of former grandeur.

Heave myself upright , flinging off the blanket, and rattle open the drawer of the cabinet. Baccie tin is still there and the matches. Today is the day. Get to fuck out of the city, out of the Model. Lay a Rizla on the cabinet and feed out a line of dry tobacco. Fingers don't work too good. Roll a fag and spark a match to light it. Suck in smoke and try not to cough. Mustn't cough. Won't stop if it starts. Old guy in next cubicle coughs and sounds like scraps of his lungs come up.

Where's my boots? Must have kicked them under the bed. Could do with new socks. Look at them. Toe nail's sticking out and holes in the heels. No use for the road.

Great day yesterday walking on the Broomielaw down by the Irish boats. Makes you want to take a trip. Could just slip up a gangway with nobody looking and sail down the Clyde. Got some VP wine and sat in the sun on the suspension bridge looking down the water and seeing the gulls swooping at garbage.

Bend and pull my boots from under the bed. Look after them. Learnt that from the CP in Spain. Wonder if the old guy next door has socks. Not going to need them for long and he stinks. Whole place stinks right enough of pish and Dettol and sweat. Right rabbit warren full of half rotten carcasses and half-dead ones like me. Five storeys high of human waste. Used to be a poor house they say. Haul on boots and tie the whangs. Get a shave in the bogs later.

Still have my clothes on so don't need to dress. Stand and tug up trousers held up with string and lift down old army greatcoat from peg, collar black with grease, buttons long gone. Check pocket for razor. All in place, carefully wrapped in cloth with brush and stick of soap. Look after the razor. Good for the Neds as well if they go for you in the street. Roll back the mattress and find that rip. Christ what a stink but there's my wallet in among the horsehair. Leather rim on my beret worn out and there's a hole in the top but beret's special. All I've got from ma uniform twenty years ago.

Hide everything 'cos these bastards here would snatch the shirt off your back.

Check next door see if he's got socks. Number 133 on the door. Dead to the world with his mouth hanging open and slavering on the pillow and lips blue with the meths. Still alive though. Lift the blanket. No socks. Soles of his feet white like wax. Christ, the mattress is soaking where he's pee'd himself. Poor old sod. Any money in his jacket? No, didn't think so. Down the corridor past all the doors peeling green paint and dented with boot marks.

Step out, blink in the sun though it's early. Hard to walk on cobbles in the yard.

Round to the caff at the suspension bridge. Mug of tea and bacon roll. Sit and watch the buses and another old guy from the Model. Crouched over his tea laced with meths. Grips his mug as if someone was going to steal it, fingers like claws coming out of army mitts. Godsakes his shoes are gaping and you can see his toes. Look after your boots, Sligo. That's what the commissar said in the brigade and he was right, squelching in the mud in Jarama. Still look after them. Neatsfoot oil.

Queer painting here right across the wall. Lots of working folk in their houses with piece bags and caps and some of them baking bread an cooking and some of them round a table holding out their hands to this man an he's giving them food. Right ghostly he is. Supposed to be Jesus I think, feeding the working folk. Could have done with him in Madrid.

Out on to Clyde Street and through to St Enoch's. Can smell

the coffee from Coopers. Up Buchanan Street and head for the canal. Wish I had socks. Get a rest on the canal bank though and then head for the railway. Good huts there for the night. Found Liverpool Jim in one last summer, been there for days, maggots crawling in his eyeholes. Stinking he was. Nothing in his pockets, some bastard been there already. Good guy, Jim, always share his bottle but not his baccie. He chewed his and spat black gobs on the floor. Suppose I should have told the polis but when you find a guy dead you tell them nothing, you keep moving, say nothing in case you get done for it.

Sligo slopes off up the street, tall, lean, beret tilted, greatcoat tied with twine, head leaning forward and hands in pockets. No-one glances in his direction or, if they do, they look away quickly, finding his appearance menacing. Unshaven, unwashed, eyes threaded red, lips blue, conjuring up images of filth and nights of oblivion spent in gutters. Dangerous, they think, unpredictable, volatile, brain minced with alcohol. Some move to the kerb to avoid him, others press against shop windows. A face in a passing tram window watches him briefly, blinks and turns away. "Vernon's Pools" below the face – win £100,000 for a penny. Into the station, nicks a couple of apples and a tomato from the kiosk and slinks away.

Sunlight on the canal and swallows swooping for flies along the water. Warm and quiet here. Take off my boots and wash my feet. Socks stick to the skin but I'll wash them too. Look after your feet, comrade. Had good socks then and boots and a Russian rifle with hammer and sickle stamped on it. A beauty. Held back the fascist bastards all day. Sunny Spain. Bollocks. Wring out the socks and let them dry on the grass. Take out the tin and roll a fag.

Something moving in the reeds there. Not like a coot. Creep over in my bare feet. Something in a sack, half-sunk. Christ it's moving! Get a stick and pull it in. Jesus it's alive. A kitten for Godsake! Some bastard chucked it in to drown.

Poor wee thing. Soaking wet and fur sticking up like a hedgehog. Rub it dry and wrap it in my beret. Mew, mew. Starving an shaking. Stick it down my front to get warm. Need to get milk or something. On with my socks and boots. There, there, wee thing. I'll get you milk. Don't know where but I'll get it and tonight we'll head for the railway and doss in one of the huts.

**

'I'll do what I can Mr Buchanan but the lad could be anywhere.'

'I do understand, constable, but I am very worried.'

'What was he wearing ?'

'Just a jersey, no jacket, short flannel trousers, socks and boots.'

'Just as well it's fine weather then. I'll have a look in some of the barns and alert the farms round about.'

'Thank you. If you do find him, please take him to the station and let me know. I don't want him returned to the Munros.'

'I see. Aye, I'll take him back and keep him till you arrive.'

'Splendid. I'll be in touch. Good night, constable,'

'Good night, sir.'

George returns to the car, throws his jacket on the passenger seat and fumbles in the pocket for his pipe. With his small penknife he scrapes out the bowl, winds down the window and knocks out the ash, wondering where Mick would hide. He has already driven round all the roads, watching for movement in the hedges or on farm roads. He is convinced that something had happened at the Munros which prompted Mick to flee. Clearly the boy had planned the escape and there must have been a reason for that. He fills his pipe, strikes a match and watches the flame dip over the bowl as he sucks.

A Jeep would be useful in the search. He had driven one in England, bouncing over the rough ground and sliding through the ruts left by the army trucks. Great fun, particularly as it was on an illicit adventure off the camp with the trainees. A motley crew, the men he trained there – journalists, salesmen, bankers, actors, playboys, tradesmen – and women too. All trained for espionage and sabotage behind the Nazi lines in France. What he had taught them could save their lives and provide crucial information to British Intelligence. It was an immense responsibility, a vital contribution. For the first time in his life he had seen himself as significant, having a real purpose. The men respected him. He had never felt like that since the war. Civilian life seemed so dull, so pedestrian, after the excitement of the war. He still found it difficult to adjust. Perhaps that's why he looked for something challenging, something useful to pay respect to the sacrifices of his students.

He had trained the agents not only to use wireless sets but also to memorise codes and complex security checks. They were warned that the German direction-finding service – *Funk Peil Dienst* – was constantly trying to find them. They had to keep moving. If they were caught, they knew that they would be in the hands of the Gestapo and probably tortured and killed. Courageous people. He admired all of them. He remembers Vera, the first woman he trained, who had worked as a milliner in Paris before the war and who, he learnt later, had been killed by lethal injection in a concentration camp. And the alluring Noor Khan, born in Russia of a Sufi father and an American mother, who was flown into France and killed in Dachau.

His students came from all over the world – Canada, Mauritius, South Africa, America, Australia and, of course, France. Regardless of their origin or class, they were his children, even if many were older than him. He felt protective of them, training them to the highest standard so that they would survive. In spite of his efforts, far too many were caught or betrayed and were killed in concentration camps. Not many Scots among them. The Brigadier, Colin Gubbins, had Scottish roots, his grandfather coming from the Isle of Mull but there was nothing in his voice to hint at a Hebridean connection. George had missed Scotland at times, surrounded by so many exotic accents off duty. He had hoped for a posting to Arisaig or Meoble or Lochailort, all training bases for special forces and all set in magnificent Highland scenery but he had been sent to Surrey.

Surrey. The gentle, wooded parish of the North Downs and the ancient manor house at the foot of the Hog's Back. He remembers the finches twittering in the ivy on the warm brick walls and the swarm of flying ants drowned on the surface of the swimming pool. He can hear the harsh voice of the sergeant putting the men through their fitness training, the constant tapping of Morse keys, the endless French conversations, the laughter of the trainees. He can hear the wind in the pines and see the heather on the ridge of the Hog's Back where he walked on free afternoons, the only place he could find which in any way resembled his native land. Nearly sixteen years ago.

He places the pipe in an ashtray, pulls out the choke and starts the car. Time to go home. One last tour of the roads in the dusk, hoping to catch a glimpse of Mick.

***

Kitten won't drink. I got milk for her and tried her with the cream off the top in a tin lid but no. Stuck cream on my finger and tried that on her lips. Lit a fire in the railway hut last night and wrapped her in my beret next to it. I was going to stuff her down my front but reckoned I might squash her in the night. Anyway fire went out in the night and the wee thing was chittering in the morning. She's not breathing too well either. Would take her to a vet but vets cost money.

Sun shinin outside. Better take her out. Bloody freezing in here. Roll a fag first though. Mind in Madrid. Fags like gold dust. Some tried nut shells and leaves off the trees and bootlaces. Working folk were good to us and got us baccie. You looked forward to parcels from home for British fags. Not that I got any but my comrades did and shared them out. You wouldn't get much for a pound a week anyhow. That was our pay. A pound a week but you got all your food and that. Soup and beans and rice, sometimes rissoles and bread. And in summer you could pick fruit off the trees, oranges, cherries and apples and olives. Good that way.

Mind the smell of blossom in the spring. Some good days right enough. Football in the sun. Spanish beat us hands down.

Lift the wee thing gently and stick her down my front. Be warm in there. Slug down the last of the milk and out on to the track. Listen for trains. Could walk on the track but the sleepers are too close together, you have to take wee short steps and that tires you out so walk on the cinders even if they're on a slope. And watch for bits of coal. Put them in the pocket for a fire at night.

Listen. There's a clink. Likely the railway walker ahead, clinking those spring things into the rails with his hammer. They're all

right usually these boys. Lonely life most of them, like ourselves.
There he is.

'Aye. Grand mornin.'

'So it is.'

'Stay in the hut last night?'

'Aye.'

'Nobody bother you?'

'No. Why?'

'Polis out lookin fer a wean.'

'On the line? Not often they come up here.'

'Naw. Polis shouted down to me from a bridge back there.'

'You know anything about cats?'

'Missus has one. Eats us outa house an home, greedy fat bastard.'

Drag the kitten out of my shirt front.

'Can't get her to drink.'

'She's had it, pal, I would say. Find her on the track?'

'No. Some bastard tried to drown her in the canal.'

'Aye. Folk are like that. Don't give a shit. I'd take it to a vet if
you wanna save it.'

'No. Vet's cost money. I'll do what I can myself.'

'Good luck well. I think it's had it. Better get on.'

'Thanks anyway.'

Polis around. Don't like that. Nosey bastards. Stuff the kitten
back in my front. Keep the wee thing warm anyway. Better she
dies in comfort.

Chapter 6

'What the fuck are you doing here?'

Didn't see him at first, boy skulking in the corner of the hut. Shit scared but a big lump of coal in his fist.

'Nothin.'

'That's no answer. On the run, eh?'

'Naw. Goin to see ma mam.'

'And she knows you're coming?'

'Aye. She'll be waitin for me.'

'Will she now? Where does she stay?'

'Glasgow.'

'You're the wean the polis are after.'

His face changes. Wee bits of defiance melt away.

'Please, mister. Don't turn us in. They'll put me back to the Munros. They'll whip me, mister. Whip me till I bleed. They tied me to a cludgie wi no clothes on. Honest. Am not lyin.'

I believe him, poor wee bastard.

'So you ran away? Is that it?'

'Couldn't take any more, mister.'

'It's you the polis are after. You can't stay here well. If the polis find you here with me, it's me they'll slap in the cells. Abducting a child they'll say.'

'Just till the morn's morn, mister. I've blisters on ma feet.'

'You think they'll heal overnight? Just like that? You're soft in the head.'

'Please.'

'Just till morning then but I get the planks. Those planks there for sleeping on. My days of dossing on the ground are long gone. Have you any grub on you?'

'Naw.'

'Stupid question.'

Reach for the kitten. Christ it's dead, just hanging there. Must have died in my front.

'Did you kill it, mister?'

'No. For fuck's sake, what would I do that for?'

'I just thought . . .'

'Well, don't think. Mind your own business.'

Go out and fling it in the bushes. Watch it spinning away in the air. Don't like this feeling inside, feeling sorry, sad. Don't want that back. That crying. Once picked up a wean in the street in Madrid. After a German bomb. Picked him up thinking he was okay but his guts fell over ma sleeve. Still alive. Looked at me like I could help him. He died in my arms. That feeling just burst out of me and I knelt down in the dust and cried like a baby. Don't want that again. Not ever. Anyways it's just a kitten for fuck's sake. Just a fucken animal. Go back in.

'You bury it, mister?'

'Aye. You go out and get some kindling, dry twigs and things and wee bits of coal if you can find them on the track. What's your name by the way?'

'Mick. What's yours?'

'Never mind mine. Just go.'

Wonder if I've a boy somewhere. My mate Jim said Deirdre was pregnant when I left. Deirdre an Bhroin, Deirdre of the Sorrows. That's why I left. Told my pals it was to fight the fascists in Spain and it was right enough but I had to get away as well. Didn't want to be a Da and she was a Tim and would never have done away with it. Maybe I've a son somewhere or a daughter even. Jesus God. Another me.

Mick comes back with a wee bundle of twigs.

'Is that all you could get? Have to do. Put them on the cinders here.'

Bit of newspaper from my pocket and scrunch it up an lay the kindling on top.

'Did you get any coal?'

'Some bits.'

'See over in the corner there's the end of a shovel. Give us it here.'

Light the fire and wait for the coal to catch. Three eggs in my pocket borrowed from a henhouse down the line. Fry them on the shovel. And two rolls.

'You boarded out, son?'

'Aye.'

'Why's that? Your Mammy not able?'

'They said that. The green lady an them.'

'You not have a Da?'

'He died when I was wee.'

'What are you going to do?'

'Find ma Ma.'

'No but after that?'

'Join the army.'

'Jesus Christ! What do you want to do that for?'

'Want to be a soldier.'

'Oh aye? I'll tell you what being a soldier's like. It's being shit scared one minute an bored to death the next. I was a soldier, son. In the Fifteenth Brigade in Spain. At Jarama. Me and my mates. One of them caught it from a shell and I crawled out the trench to help him but he wasn't there. Not in one piece anyway. Bits of him all over the place. When I crawled back there was this other man just sitting there but he had no head just a mess of bloody flesh at his collar. That's what it's like. Only twenty four out of a hundred and six Brigaders came out of Brunete. And I caught one too. A bang like you'd been hit by a train and then black. At first I thought I was on my face in the mud an then I knew what it was. I was buried, son. Under the sod and alive and I couldn't move. Scared? Christ I thought it was the end. Mud in my mouth an up my nose and pain in my side like a lion was chewing me. Here, son, here's eggs for you and a roll. Don't be a soldier. Anything but a soldier. By the time you're old enough they'll maybe stop the call up and, if you get the call, just fuck off to the wilds. Up north or away to France. Just disappear.'

'Did you ever shoot anybody?'

'You eat your eggs and never mind that. I'll go and hunt for coal.'

Under the mud I was. When they dug me out I was sobbing like a wife at a funeral. Took me to hospital, screaming on the lorry with a big black hole in my side. Annie Murray. Won't forget her. A nurse from Fife. Braver than most men and calm and kind. Only fell out once when I shouted at this Italian in another bed.

Hate fucken Eyeties. Their planes dropped wee chocolate boxes with hand bombs in them for the children to pick up. Blew up in their faces. I swore at that Eyetie and Annie gave me a row. Felt bad about it after cos the poor bastard died that night.

Wonder where she is now, Annie Murray. Don't think she'd think much of me and the way I live. Came back from the Big War, back from Palestine, and couldn't get a job. Soon as they heard I'd been in Spain they turned me down. Must be a commie him. A commie for fuck's sake. Don't get me wrong. The commies in the Brigade were good guys and the commissar gave his life for the cause. But I was there to fight the fascists not to listen to long boring speeches about politics. Anyway, no work after the war.

'Thanks, mister.'

'What?'

'Thanks for the eggs.'

'Need your food, son, if you're running from the polis.'

'I've no money.'

'Don't need money. Watch for hen houses by the track and bread vans in the early morning down in the streets. Get milk there too at the doors.'

There they are in a small hut made of sleepers with a crumbling brick chimney. Smoke curls slowly into the summer dusk. Sligo rolls a fag on his knee as he sits by the fire. Mick sits on the floor, gazing into the coals, his hands clasped round his bare knees. They could be father and son. As the light fades, a cold breeze sweeps along the track, funnelled between the steep banks.

'Where you goin tomorra, mister?'

'Don't know yet.'

'Can I come with you?'

'No. You're looking for your Ma, mind.'

'Am feart o the polis.'

'Look, son. I'll show you how to get to Glasgow without them seeing but that's it. End of story. Right?'

'Right.'

'Where's your Ma anyway?'

'Gorbals.'

'Aye but where?'

'Don't know what it's called but I mind the street.'

'You haven't a fucken clue, have you?'

'Aye I do. I'll find her.'

'Maybe. You'd better get some sleep. Here take my coat an wrap yourself in it.

It'll get cold when the coals die down.'

I doss down on the planks. Middle of the night a train comes roaring past, flames belching from its funnel. Boy yells in fright and starts running about in the dark.

'Fuck's sake, son.'

Grab his arm and he lashes out at my face.

'Son, son. Calm down. It's me. It's me. It's only a train.'

'Jesus Christ. I didnae do it. Please. I didnae.'

'You're okay, son. Calm down. No-one's going to hurt you.'

He calms down and starts to greet.

'Fuck's sake, son. Don't greet. No need for that. You're okay, You're safe.'

He rolls himself in my coat and sobs himself to sleep. Poor wee mite. If I'd the bastards here who leathered him, I'd slit their fucken throats.

Chapter 7
MICK

Don't know why he did that. Took me all the way to the river. Never said nuthin when he left. Got us a mug a tea an a roll in the caff, stood up an whirled away like he was in a hurry. Wonder if it's all stories, him bein a soldier an that. Doesn't look like a soldier.

Was good to me tho. I went across the suspension bridge and into the Gorbals. Just can't mind where we were with ma Mam. Streets look all the same. Been up hunerds o closes askin for her. Women open the door a wee chink an shake their heads an say nothin. One auld guy came out an smacked me in the mouth an tellt me to fuck off. Only askin for ma Mam. Legs are gettin sore now, up and down all they stairs, an guts think ma throat's cut. Starvin. Maybe I could nick somethin outa that Paki shop.

Comin down the stair this woman was sittin on the bottom step wi her hand on a pram handle.

'Have you seen my Ma? Bridget Crossan.'

'Naw, son. No Bridget Crossan in this close. Don't know the name either. Listen, son, gies a han wi the pram up the stair, will ye? I cannae make it an the kids cannae hear me shoutin.'

'Aye, sure.'

She gets up and starts pullin an I start pushin. Bump.Bump. She's awfu thin an pechin at every step. Stops an leans on the wa on the first landin.

'You awright Missus?'

'Aye, fine. Fine, son.'

We goes another lot a stairs and she starts coughin like a sick cow, like she was goin to puke. I stands there waitin, thinkin she goin to snuff it but she stops in the end an goes on up.

We comes to her place an the door's open an she goes in an I'm left wi the pram. She comes back out.

'Come in, son. Bring it in.'

Four kids. Wee one just in a vest wi ketchup on the front an his wee willie pokin out. Girl in a dress an bare legs wi mud on her knees. Boy wi head shaved an blue stuff all over it. Looks like the Mekon. Boy bit youngern me wi trousers on an socks wi no toes. Lookin at me like he was goin to burst ma nose. Just let him try. Big girl takes the pram off me. Doesn't even say nuthin.

Woman takes bread outa the pram an cuts slices on the table an clarts them wi jam an gives pieces to the kids. She makes me a piece too.

'Here son. For helpin me up the stair.'

'Thanks missus.'

'Mary wet some tea in the big pot.'

'We've nae milk Ma.'

'Just have to do without then. Tea's fine an there's sugar there.'

Big girl fills the kettle at the sink an goes over to the fire.

'Need coal, Ma, or wood or somethin. Fire's near out.'

The ashes are spillin out onto the floor an Mary pushes them in wi her shoe.

'Can I stay here the night, missus?' I says.

'Naw,' says Mary, 'there's nae room.'

'He's lookin for his Ma for God's sake. Leave him alone, Mary. Where were you last night, son?'

'In a hut on the railway.'

'Have you run from a home or somethin?'

'Naw. I was stayin wi' ma Da in Dundee an he took ill an died an am lookin for my Ma to stay wi her'

'What did you call her again?'

'Bridget Crossan.'

'Not about here, son. Mary, have you heard tell o Bridget Crossan?'

'No.'

'Don't mind her, son. She's aye crabbit. Anyways you can stay but you'll have to sleep on ma coat on the floor. John, you go out an see if you can find some coal. Take this yin with you. What's your name, son?'

'Mick.'

'Take Mick with you. Get coal or bitsa wood. He'll help you carry them.'

John digs under the bed an gets his shoes an puts them on. Near dark now on the stair.

'Got any fags?' he says.

'Naw.'

Never says about the ten shillin.

'Where'll we get coal about here? No railway here.'

'Round at the stables. Whiles they leave bits on the cart an drop them by the shed.'

We goes round an right enough there are bitsa coal on the cobbles. I goes over to the shed an there's a big heavy padlock on the door so I goes round the back to see if there's a way in an there's a windae high up.

'Nae use,' he says. 'Duffy keeps a fucken big dug in there. I tried.'

We fills our pockets wi bits and go back.

'Good lads,' she says.

'Is that all?' says Mary.

Enough to get the fire goin an get some tea.

The crowded tenements at night are never quiet. The streets outside echo with voices, some in anger, some in snatches of song, some in despair. Even as the gas lights behind the windows snuff out one after another, the closes murmur and move. A child coughs ceaselessly in its sleep, cats screech among the refuse in the back yards, a mother moans in a box bed beside her kids as she scratches her bites, a bread van rattles over the cobbles and, in the distance, a train clatters over a railway bridge. The river rings with the scream of caulkers' grinders, metal to metal on ship's plates in the yards, and the water glitters blue with the flashes of welding. A blanket of smoke, rising from a multitude of chimneys, hangs over the city, muffling the sounds and reflecting the glow of streetlights and iron furnaces. You can taste the sulphur on your tongue.

Mary sweats beside her mother and the children at her feet in the only bed. Enclosed in the narrow space around it, the bed reeks of paraffin rubbed on the wood to kill the lice. Mick sleeps on the bare floorboards wrapped in a coat. The fire smoulders in the grate, warming the black kettle beside it. The single tap in the sink drips on to a plate smeared with jam. Under the table a mouse nibbles at breadcrumbs.

I wakes up burstin for a pee but don't know where to go. They're still asleep too. I squeeze ma legs together but it's no use. I'll have to ask. I fling off the coat an goes to the bed.

'Missus,' I says but she doesna move. Jesus I'll have to shake her.

'Missus,' I says an touch her arm. Christ she leaps up wi her eyes starin.

'Who are you? What are doin in ma hoose?'

'Mick, Missus. You said I could stay.'

'O God aye. I forgot.'

'Where's the cludgie, Missus? I need a pee.'

'Key's by the sink there. Outside an on your left.'

I goes out to the stair and finds the cludgie. Thank God. Pee rattles on the newspaper in the cludgie. Last in here never pulled the chain. Dirty bastard.

I goes back an she's up countin coins on the table.

'Mary, get up an go an get us a plain loaf an a jar o jam.'

Mary pulls the curtain across the box bed so's I can't see her dressin.

'Have to keep some for the rent. Factor comes the day an I'm a week behind.'

'I'll give you rent, missus, if you'll let me stay till I find ma Mam.'

'Don't be daft, son. How would a skelf like you pay rent?'

'I'll find a job.'

'Good of you, son, but we'll manage.'

Mary comes out an puts on her shoes. Her Ma gives her money an she goes out.

I goes after her an takes out the ten shillin.

'Get us ten Woodbine an two loaves an butter an jam an sausages an eggs.'

'Wherdya get that, Mick? You stole it, didn't ya?'

'I did not. Ma Da gave it us.'

'You're a liar. I know you are.'

'Am not. It's mine. Go on for fuck's sake before I take it back.'

'They folk in the shop'll ask where I got it.'

'Say your Ma's got a lodger.'

She goes down the stair. I like the way her hair bounces on her frock.

'Don't forget ma fags,' I shouts down the close.

I goes back in an stands by the sink.

'Where did yous Ma stay?' she says.

'I can't mind the street but I'll know the place when I see it.'

'Definitely in the Gorbals?'

'Aye. I mind the bridge, the bridge you walk over.'

'I'll ask about for you. Somebody must know, eh? What's she look like?'

'Beautiful. Black hair an blue eyes an a scarf wi' shamrocks an shoes wi wee bows.'

'You're fond o' your Ma. Eh?'

'Aye'

Jesus ma eyes get all wet. What a jessie. I go an look out the window.

Mary comes back with the stuff in a bag.

'Jesus, Mary ! Wheredya get that? You can't get that on tick ! For God's sake.'

'It's him, Ma. He gave me ten shillin'.'

'Didya, Mick?'

'Aye. Ma Da gave it me an I'll give you some for rent.'

'God love you,son. A few shillin won't go far. You keep that tae yersel. We'll get by. You can stay here till you find yer Ma. We'll have a fry an Mary'll take you roun tae Mrs Lundy in Bedford Street see if you can get a bit mattress or somethin.'

'No frae her, Ma. It'll be crawlin. I'll get somethin frae ma work.'

'Nonsense. Mrs Lundy's stuff's been cleaned. An don't be takin anythin frae your work. None o that.'

'Can you get me a job at your work?' I says to Mary.

'Don't be daft. It's all women. I work in the hair factory. Makin mattresses.'

'Mary, get they weans ready fer the school while I make a fry.'

We're sittin at the table an this priest comes to the door. Bad news. Nosey bastards they priests.

'Good morning, Mrs Doyle. I was visiting poor Mrs Healey upstairs. Very poorly she is. I haven't seen you at mass Mrs Doyle nor you, Mary, and I was worried for you.'

'I'm grand thank you father. We'll be there next Sunday.'

'I think you said that last time I called, Mrs Doyle, and the time before that.'

'I've plenty tae think about feedin these weans.'

'Of course you have. But we must look after out immortal souls as well. And who is this young man? You have a lodger, Mrs Doyle?'

'Ma cousin's boy just visiting. No lodger father.'

'What cousin is that now? Did I meet her at the funeral at all?'

'No. She's in Dundee. She couldn't come.'

'That's a shame. A long way right enough. Did you come on your own, young man? What's your name by the way?'

'Robert, father. I came on the train.'

'Now that's an adventure and not cheap either.'

'Ma Da paid.'

'I hope you kept the ticket, son, the return ticket. You'll still have that, eh?'

'Aye.'

'Father,' says Mary, 'I've tae get dressed for work and get the weans dressed for school.'

'Of course, Mary. You're a grand girl, looking after the children and helping your mother. I'll go and leave you in peace. I hope I'll see you all in Mass and you too Robert. You'll be in the school, no doubt, so I'll see you there. What's your second name?'

'O'Donnell, father.'

'O'Donnell is it? A good Irish name that. The whole of the clan must live in the city there's so many of them. Well, I'll be on my way. God bless you all.'

He goes out an Mary smiles at me.

'You'll go the bad fire, you. O'Donnell!'

'Will he tell about me?'

'Naw. There's things we could tell about him.'

Chapter 8

George parks his car outside the police station in Oxford Street, carefully locks the door and glances up to admire the carvings on the red sandstone building.

'Rather ostentatious for the Gorbals,' he mutters.

He pushes open the distinctly unwelcoming heavy oak door and steps in to reception.

The constable behind the desk does not look up. George watches him writing painfully in the ledger, the pen gripped like a weapon in his massive fingers. They would be happier wielding a spanner. The frown portrays intense concentration and effort. George feels for him.

'What can I do for you, sir?' he says eventually.

'Good morning, constable. I sent in a report concerning a boy missing from a farm in Fife, one of my charges.'

'Can I have your name, sir?'

'Yes, sorry. I should have introduced myself. George Buchanan, Children's Officer.'

'If he was in Fife, is that not Fife's business?'

'He is originally from here and we have reason to believe that he will return to the Gorbals to find his mother.'

'Trying to find anyone in this rabbit warren is a major task if they don't want to be found. How long has the lad been missing?'

'Three weeks now.'

'Long time on the run. He'll be stealing food no doubt. Unless he's found his mother that is. What's she called?'

'Bridget Crossan. Last heard of in Crown Street.'

'Don't know the name. A few Crossans around but no Bridget I can think of. With a name like that she'll be a Catholic I suppose. Have you asked the priests?'

'Not yet. I'm hoping to call on them today.'

'What did she work at? Did she have steady work like?'

'No. Took in washing, scrubbed floors, anything like that.

Wherever she could find work. Not a slacker. Worked her fingers to the bone.'

'Not a prostitute then? Plenty of women take to that.'

'No. Unless she's been forced into it recently.'

'If she's been cautioned for soliciting or arrested, we'll have a record. That could help.'

'Yes, of course. Could you have a look?'

'That'll take time. I tell you what. I'll go and ask the boys in the back if they know anything. Take a seat, sir.'

George sits on the bench, its seat torn and singed with cigarette burns. He takes out his pipe and matches and lights the bowl. He wonders if Bridget could have taken to prostitution and what effect that would have on Mick were he to discover it. He knew that many women took to the streets, some in desperation, others out of choice. He had seen the girls around the late-night coffee stalls in the centre of town and met the middle-class women from the Women's Help Society determined to reform them. He disliked the way these crusaders accompanied plain-clothes officers as they dealt with the girls and took note of their personal details, a clear violation of their freedom. A bit like the collaborators who betrayed his trainee operators in France. He had read that one of the leading ladies had tried to persuade the Wolfenden committee to have prostitutes imprisoned for sixty days. Her views annoyed him so much that he had written to the chairman himself.

'I'm afraid that none of the boys have heard of Bridget Crossan, recently, sir. Constable MacArthur thinks he remembers a woman by that name in Crown Street some time ago but he's sure she left for Ireland. You could try the Women's Help or Salvation Army. And your report about the boy is being handled by Sergeant Duffy. He won't be in the office till the afternoon. If you would like to call back, he may have some information but I'm afraid we get hundreds of missing children in this division. Wouldn't hold your breath.'

'Thanks anyway, constable. I think I will take a walk and call back. I'm keen to find the boy. He's been very badly treated and deserves some help. I hate to think of him sleeping in a close or an outside toilet somewhere.'

'Like many others.'

'Indeed. I'll be back. Thank you for your help.'

George steps out, knocks his pipe against the wall and heads for Crown Street where Mick's mother was living when last seen by officials. He finds the doorway between a bookmaker's and a baker's shop, its rich scent tempting him to walk in and buy a couple of fresh rolls. He resists, however, noticing the Rainbow café further up the street. He looks up at the soot-black four-storey tenement above the line of shops and wonders how women manage the trek to the top floor. Hearing children's voices in the back court, he wanders through the tunnel.

The dry weather has baked the mud to a hard crust and the wind is blowing dust from the piles of ash. Flies swarm above the bins and the stench of decay is overpowering. Some children are playing in the sun, the girls having a pretend tea-party with broken cups on a discarded tea-chest, the boys taking turns on top of a barrel as they roll it across the yard.

As he approaches the girls they step back, one still holding a spoutless teapot.

'Good morning, young ladies. Can I have a cup of tea?'

'Cost ya thruppence, mister,' the one with the teapot says.

He produces a three-penny bit and holds it up.

'Thrupence for tea and if you can tell me where Bridget Crossan lives.'

'Up there,' she says, pointing to a top floor window behind him.

Too quick a response to be truthful.

'Has she a boy Mick? Older than you.'

'There's no Mick in our close,' says one of the others.

'Shut up you!'

'Aye she has, mister. She's a liar.'

'Can I have my tea?' He hands her the coin.

She pretends to pour into one of the filthy cups.

'Do you take sugar an milk?'

'Two sugars and a drop of milk.'

She spoons imaginary sugar into the cup, pours in milk and hands it to him. He pretends to drink.

'Good cup of tea. Thanks.'

He goes over to the boys. The barrel stops rolling and one of them jumps off.

'Has anyone seen Mick – Mick Crossan?'

They shake their heads.

He knows that, even if they had, they would not say. He was one of the enemy. They stand there in their short trousers silently waiting for him to leave. Pointless, he decides and walks back. Time for lunch.

Three boys are playing marbles in the street as he emerges from the close. The oldest of them should be at school and he is tempted to ask him about Mick but decides to avoid the inevitable glare of contempt and deceitful reply. He hears him shout 'Sheevies' triumphantly as he walks away.

He has a sandwich and a tepid coffee in the Rainbow café and walks down to the river. The sour taste of the coffee lingers in his mouth. Camp coffee with chicory, that dreadful reminder of the war. He leans on the rail of the suspension bridge, watching a line of flotsam winding its way toward the sea. He thinks of Mick and the Munros. He should have intervened earlier when his intuition told him that things were not as they seemed. Yet he would have had to justify Mick's removal with evidence and that was not substantial. The Munros were just the kind of people to complain to the Committee. Mick's flight from the farm and Mrs Munro's outrageous behaviour were sufficient reason for concern but came too late. What an appalling woman she was. In some ways he hoped that Mick did find his mother. The reunion would bring the boy some happiness. Perhaps he shouldn't try too hard to find him. Yet, if she had left for Ireland, the boy might be starving and sleeping in closes. He would have to continue the search.

He was not looking forward to his meeting with a parish priest. Too many of them were evasive, equivocal and untrustworthy. By no means all of them for some were charming, helpful and humorous. He did recognise that his strict Presbyterian background bred a distrust of Catholic clergy and he did his best to overcome it but he tended to dislike them until he was forced into a reassessment. Their treatment of orphan children always worried him. He knew of one orphanage where the children had to sleep with their arms crossed over their chests and were thrashed for failing to comply. Another grim, castellated institution about which there were stories of barbaric punishments administered by sadistic nuns in the name of God, any investigation of such chastisement being met with outraged denial. He was determined to keep Mick or any of his charges out of these institutions.

He returns to the police station.

'Ah Mr Buchanan. I'll just get the sergeant. Take a seat.'

Sergeant Duffy comes through and sits beside him. He is surprised to find such a diminutive policeman in the Gorbals, expecting the force there to consist of sturdy Highlanders or Irishmen. Still, the small man exudes an air of authority and competence.

'Good afternoon, sir. I have your report and I've made some enquiries but I'm afraid we've been unable to find any trace of your boy. We have had to divert some of our men to the Burnside murders so we're a bit short of staff. I understand you're to see the priest and that's probably the best course of action. Father Begley is your man. He takes a great interest in the youngster around here. In the meantime we will keep an eye out for him.'

'Thank you, sergeant. I know you're all very busy and one wee boy missing can't be priority but I am worried about him and would hate to see him come to any harm.'

'Of course, sir. Try Father Begley. At St Luke's in Ballater Street.'

With that, he rises and scuttles away.

George takes the car round to St Luke's. The playground in front of the school is blossoming brightly with girls skipping, laughing, chanting and playing peever. They all ignore him as he walks through the playground to the priests' house behind and knocks the door. A small red-haired man eventually appears, his breath scented with alcohol and his collar awry.

'Good afternoon. I'm looking for Father Begley.'

'Well, you won't have to look far. I'm Father Begley, though some of my flock have other less seemly names for me. How can I help?'

'I'm George Buchanan, a Children's Officer. I'm looking for a lad who has absconded from a placement in Fife and I think he may have come to this parish as his mother used to live in Crown Street.'

'Well now. I was in Crown Street this morning. What is his mother's name? Let's start with that.'

'Bridget Crossan.'

'No-one like that in Crown Street that I know of. She could be a Protestant of course, though with that name I think she'll be one of ours.'

'In her records she claims to be Roman Catholic.'

'Sure some of them just say the first thing that comes into their heads and are no more Catholic than Billy Simpson of Rangers. But hang on now. I remember there was a Bridget Crossan but she lived in Warwick Street. She had a wee girl who was taken from her – thought to be in moral danger – and sent to Smyllum Park in Lanark and then to Canada. The woman herself was not fit to look after her.'

'That's strange. There's no mention of that in our records.'

'It may not be the same person. Anyway, we arranged the whole thing.'

'I see.'

'You know, now that I think about it, there is a youngster who has just appeared in one of our families – rather shifty young man. Said his name was Robert O'Donnell but I'm sure he was lying. I wonder if that could be your man. Leave this with me and I'll take a wee walk round there. I don't like to think of him in that family. There's an attractive young daughter there and very little room in the house. They all sleep together in the one bed and never come to Mass. Leave me your phone number, Mr Buchanan, and I'll give you a ring.'

'That's very good of you.'

'Anything to help.'

'I'll be off then. Goodbye and thank you.'

'Goodbye and God bless.'

Chapter 9
MICK

'Mary!' she shouts out the window to the back court, 'come up here!'

Kathleen they ca her, Mary's Ma. She's bundlin a pile o washin intae the pram wi a fag hangin in her mouth an the fags have made her hair a sorta yella above her eye.

'Mick, will you gie Mary a han doon the stair so as the pram doesnae run away wi her?'

'Sure, Missus.'

She's let me stay till I find ma Ma an I buys bread an jam an porridge for the breakfast. I got a ham bone from the butcher an she made soup wi lentils an peas.

Mary comes pechin up the stair.

'What, Ma? I wish you wouldn't yell out at me like that. Its embarrassin.'

'I clean forgot I booked a place at the steamie, Mary. Can you take the washin over for me? I've got tae get this fire goin. Mick'll gie you a han doon the stair.'

'I don't need a hand.'

'Don't be daft. I don't want the washin spilt all over the stair.'

I goes in front o the pram wi ma back to it and down we goes. Bump, bump,bump.

We gets to the bottom and she says,

'I'm fine now. You can go back up.'

'Do you want a fag?'

'Well, don't you tell my Ma.'

I gets out ma Woodbine and light up

'Where can I get a job here?'

'A job! You should be at school. They'll find out you know.'

'Never goin back. I need a job tho.'

No. Never goin back an never back to Munro's nor any place like it. Run an run an they'll never get me. Run tae London or away up north intae the mountains or the forests. Never get me.

Sooner a gas oven than go back.

'You could ask the milkman. Only thing is you have to be up at the crack o day. He takes on boys or the Co-op bread van or you could go roun the doors askin if you can run messages an there's a place under the arches where they break up old furniture an sell it for sticks. But you should be at school. You'll never get anywhere if you don't go, ma Da says that.'

'Where's he anyway?'

'Away on the Hydro schemes somewhere up north. Never here. Well, here a coupla years ago. Sends postal orders when he remembers an that's not often. Where's yours?'

'Dead. Ma says he was at sea. Never seen him much.'

'Ma uncle's at sea too wi Blue Funnel. His weans never see him either. Anyways I'd better go or Ma'll be ragin.'

'I'll come wi you.'

'Don't be stupit, it's a wimen. They'd jist laugh. Never been tae a steamie?'

'Naw. Niver.'

'No wi yer Ma?'

'Naw. Wasn't wi ma Ma that often. In homes mostly.'

'Oh. Well, look, ye can come an wait outside.'

I like her blue eyes an the way she holds her fag like a film star an tilts her head back when she smokes. She goes in front of me wi the pram an I like the bare legs an her heel all rubbed wi her shoe. I'd like tae put ma arm round her but she might tell me tae fuck off. You can never tell wi girls. I've never seen one nude. Maybe in they books like 'Men Only' or that other one wi the funny name an then they're sort of misty in the bits you want to see.

Pictures make you want to do it yersel. 'Self-abuse' the priests called it in the home. Told you your brain leaked away when you did it in bed an they flogged you if you were caught.

One o them tried it on wi Davey but Davey wisnae feart. Smacked him in the teeth.

He got leathered till he bled but the bastard never came near him again.

'Where dae I go for the milk run?'

'Up tae the river an along. Scottish Farmers. Yer not goin now are ye?'

'Aye.'

'Washin'll be awfu heavy comin back.'

'I'll get you at the steamie.'

I runs up the street an along tae the dairy an sees milk floats in a yard. There's a big man heavin crates inside the gate.

'Any chance of a job, mister?'

He stops an looks at me.

'What age are you, son?'

'Fifteen.'

He laughs.

'An I'm a hundred and one. Yer a bluddy liar. Look, see that old guy wi the horse an cart? Go an ask him. He takes on youngsters.'

I goes over tae the old man an he's shovin a nose bag on tae the horse.

'Any chance of a job, mister?'

He says nuthin. Mebbe he's deaf so I says it again.

'O heard ye the first time, son. What age are ye?'

'Fifteen.'

'I only take on men who are honest.'

'OK, I'm thirteen.'

'That's a bit nearer the truth. You're still at school then?'

'Aye.'

'An which one is that?'

I can't mind the name o Mary's so I says the one along the road.

'St Luke's.'

'A Tim then, eh?'

'Aye.'

'Can't help that I suppose. What's your name, son?'

'Patrick. Patrick McMahon.'

'Well, Paddy. If I take you on, ye'll have to be in the yard at five thirty, feed the horse, muck out the stable, load the cart an that's before you start work.'

'How much do you pay, mister?'

'Never mind that. You turn up an I'll see at the end o the week what you're worth.'

'Right, mister. I'll be there the morn's mornin an I'll show you I can work.'

I runs back tae the steamie, skippin every square on the

pavement like I was a lassie. I goes in an I don't care. Rows o wimen in pinnies an big tin basins bangin oan they big tub things birlin an shoutin an Christ ye cannae hear yersel speak. What a fucken racket.

'Come tae wash yer panties, son?' shouts one o them.

I says nuthin. I sees Mary at the top loadin wet washin intae the pram an gives her a hand.

'I gotta job,' I shouts.

'Oh aye?'

'Aye, right enough. Wi the milk cart.'

'Wait till we get oota here. I cannae hear you right.'

We loads the pram an she pulls it out intae the street.

'Whose gonna waken ye? No be me anyway.'

'Dunno. Maybe I'll get a clock or somethin. Or maybe I'll sleep in the stable.'

'Wi the horses? They'll never let ye do that.'

'Maybe I'll not let on.'

'Don't be daft. They'll find oot an ca the polis.'

We walks back an I gie her a hand up the stair. Christ the prams heavy. We're both fair wabbit at the top.

'Och Mick,' says Kathleen, 'that's awfu good o you. I'll make a cuppa tea.'

'Mick's gotta job, Ma.'

'Have you, Mick?'

'Aye. Wi the milk cart but I've to be in the yard by half five.'

'In the name of God that's the middle o the night. Never mind, though, we'll manage. I'll get ye up. We'll get a clock on tick just in case.'

Mary got a clock, a yella thing wi keys on the back, an we wound it up last night an set it beside me on the floor. Jesus it rang all right. Woke half the close. Didn't Kathleen, though. I dressed an took ma boots an creeped down the stair in ma stockin soles.

Here I am at the milk yard an no sign o the man. I spark up a fag an wait. An wait.

I hears the horse inside makin that shiverin sound an I lifts the bar an goes intae the stable.

Jesus its huge if you're near it. It looks back at me with they big

54

eyes like black snooker balls. Disnae like me I think. Scrapes a hoof on the cobbles. 'Feed it' he said. What with?

I look round but can see nuthin tae feed it.

'Put that fag out!'

Christ Jesus what a fright. The man comes in the door and smacks me one on the ear. Near knocks ma head off.

'Never smoke in here. The whole bloody place could go up in smoke.'

'Sorry mister. Awfu sorry. I won't do it again.'

'Too bloody right you won't. Now see that big kist there? Open it an fill that wee pail wi some bruised oats an tim them into her trough.'

I does as he says. I creeps round in front of her. Jesus she nudges ma ear wi yon big, soft hairy lips. God's sake She's so big am shittin myself but she gets tore into the oats as soon as I cowp them intae her trough.

'When she's busy eating you can get the barra an muck out.'

'I can do that, mister. I was on a farm. Where's the midden?'

'Just see an not prick her leg wi' the fork or you'll get a right clatter wi her hoof.'

After that he lifts this big collar thing an turns it upside down an shoves it over her head.

'You watch carefully, son, so's you can get her yoked.'

He gets a the belts on an buckles done up an straps over her head an things in her mouth an backs her out. Her shoes clatter on the cobbles an he backs her intae the trams. She's hitched up an he drives her cart over tae the loadin bank.

'Right boy. Now the work starts. We load they crates o milk on the cart.'

Jesus they're heavy. Can hardly lift them. He flings them round as if they were feather pillas. But he's soon sweating' under his bunnet an its dreepin aff his nose.

'C'mon boy. Put yer back into it or we'll be here all day.'

Across the yard there's men loadin a milk van, one o them wi a motor. Whole place smells o sour milk.

We loads up an off we go. I sits up beside him on the cart like one o they men on a stagecoach waitin for the Injuns. Wish I had a gun on my knee an one o they cowboy hats.

Wish Mary could see me but she'll still be in bed likely.

We goes out past the closes tae the houses.

'Now, son. I'll tell you how many bottles fer each house. Take them up an bring back the empties an put them in the crates. Some folk'll leave a note to say how many. Whatever they say goes.'

We goes on an on till all the milk's gone.

'Time for a wee rest' he says, 'See that nosebag. Hang it over her ears.'

He sits back an takes out his pipe an lights up. He has this tin top wi holes fittin over the top.

'Where are you stayin, son?'

'Crown Street.'

'Oh aye? My son's in Crown Street. Which close are you in?'

'I can't mind the number.'

'You can't mind the number! What's your Da's name then?'

'Da's dead. Stay wi cousins. They've no Da neither.'

'God's sake, an what's their Ma's name?'

'Kathleen.'

'Kathleen what? Christ its like pullin teeth.'

'Don't know her second name.'

'Do you ever tell the truth, son?'

'I am. Ma Dad died two weeks back in Dundee an he sent me here. I'm new here.'

'Aye well find out your aunt's name. I want to know. I need to know who you are.'

'I will, mister. I promise I will.'

We heads back tae the yard an he louses the horse an takes off all the straps an things.

'You watch how to take off her bridle an the bit out of her mouth so's you can do it.'

Jesus I don't like the look o' they big yella teeth an the way she slavers.

'Now get up that ladder into the loft and throw down a bale o hay.'

I runs up the ladder and grabs a bale by the twine an tosses it down.

'Come down here for God's sake. Don't stand up there like dummy.'

I hurries down like he says and skelps ma knee on the ladder.

'Now look. Cut the twine just by the knot like this and then hang it up there wi the rest, see. I make mats out o them.'

I looks up an there's a big bundle o' twines all neat an hangin the same way.

'Then you throw her two slaps o hay, no moren that, right? And when she's eatin you brush her down wi that brush there. Brush her till she shines and then you can go.'

'Same time tomorra, mister? Did I do okay?'

'Same time tomorrow and see and ask your aunt her name. I want to know who she is.'

Chapter 10

'Listen to this,' George says from behind his newspaper.

His wife does not look up from the page of 'Woman's Own'.

'This is splendid. The TB campaign in Glasgow. It says here that a letter has been sent to every household in Glasgow inviting people to a free X Ray in the city centre. There's been dedication services in the Cathedral, St Andrew's church and all the synagogues. A team of athletes bearing torches left George Square for all thirty seven wards of the city. An illuminated tram toured the city with recordings of Jimmy Logan singing 'An X Ray For Me' and, for the youngsters, an X Ray Rock. Every person attending for an X Ray will get a badge with random gifts of chickens and cigarettes.'

'Cigarettes? For TB patients?'

'I think that will be for those who are clear, dear. The names of those attending will be placed in a ballot for a prize of an Austin 35 car.'

'I imagine there will be those who attend several times then.'

'Don't be so cynical. I think it is an excellent scheme. Anything that reduces the scourge of TB has to be a blessing.'

'And how much is this to cost?'

'Let me see. I don't think it says. Oh yes. Here. Twenty thousand pounds.'

'Good grief! Perhaps they could have saved on all those fripperies.'

'If it saves a few lives, it will be worth every penny. I wonder if that boy Mick and his mother will turn up. I might make enquiries.'

'Been rather a long time. They might have left Glasgow long ago.'

'True. Still, worth a try. They are prime candidates for TB, especially the mother, given the squalor in which they lived.'

'Cousin Jane didn't live in squalor. Quite the opposite. Seven years flat on her back in that hospital, the back of her head as bald as an onion and her nose always choked. They had to scrape her sinuses to keep them clear. Snorting like a sow and barely able to talk. I could scarcely find the strength to visit her and watch her suffer. I know that sounds dreadful but I detested those visits. Always thinking that I might catch it too. Most uncharitable.'

'Yes, I remember. You did go though and she lived for those visits.'

'So many died. She used to lie waiting for the trolley to come round for the corpses. The 'pan loaf' they called it for some reason. Must have been like a nightmare, listening to the squeak of the trolley and thinking that you would be the next victim.'

'Terrifying.'

George lays down his paper and reaches for his pipe.

'Mr Menzies up the road has just bought one,' she says.

'What?'

'An Austin.'

'Oh. I couldn't think what you were talking about. He must have come into some money. They're more than £500.'

'An improvement on your Popular anyway.'

'I'm quite happy with it. I have no wish to impress my neighbours.'

He sits back and remembers with horror his visit to his brother in Robroyston hospital before the war. Vast, sprawling ranks of single-storey buildings like a small town set in the countryside north of Glasgow. There was even a factory chimney with a plume of black smoke which he assumed was a laundry.

No-one spoke on the bus, each locked in their trepidation as they prepared themselves for the visit to their relatives or friends and each of them keen to hide their connection to TB. Fear of the disease and the stigma attached to it was widespread. He remembers the long walk from the gate, his new shoes pinching his feet so that he was quite lame by the time he found the right building. Outside under a glass roof a row of beds stretched the whole length of the veranda with patients happed up in a variety of headgear to keep themselves warm. His brother was not with them.

He found him inside, his scarlet cheeks set incongruously in a deathly pale face as if they had been powdered with rouge. He was clearly in pain, so much so that George could not try to cheerful.

'How are you, Jack?' was all he could find to say.

'I was fine till yesterday.'

'What happened?'

'Ask the nurse. I haven't the strength.'

The nurse took him aside and explained that the doctor had decided to try Artificial Pneumothorax, a technique which involved injecting air into the chest cavity through the ribs so that the lung collapses.

'Good God! Sounds dreadful.'

'We do give them a local anaesthetic.'

'Jack's in pain today. Who decided to do this?'

'Doctor Flynn.'

'I'd like to speak to him.'

'He's very busy.'

'I would like to speak to him, nevertheless. I have come a long way to see my brother.'

Even then he did not like to be thwarted by minor figures of authority.

She hesitated but eventually turned away and marched down the ward, her heels clicking crossly on the polished floor. She returned with the doctor, a man clearly unused to being summoned.

'This is Jack's brother,' she said.

'Ah yes. I can see the resemblance. Your brother is making good progress.'

'Good afternoon, doctor. I'm worried about this procedure. Can you explain to me how it helps?'

'Your brother was finding it increasingly difficult to breathe so we felt that a collapse of the left lung in order to rest it might help.'

'Is there not a grave risk attached to that?'

'There is always a risk of infection but the equipment is scrupulously sterilised and the instruments used are extremely accurate. Let me show you.'

He took him to the end of the ward and showed him a patient undergoing the treatment. The victim was in an extraordinary position, lying on his side with an arm raised above his head and a pillow under his chest to lift it into an arc. He was lying there like a side of meat in a butcher's shop. The needle had been inserted through his ribs and a rubber tube led to a set of instruments with a chrome measuring gauge.

'See, the patient is in no pain.'

'And afterwards?'

'Slight discomfort, no more.'

'My brother is in pain.'

'In his case the first incision did not work so we had to repeat the procedure in a different part of the chest. I expect it is the first incision that is causing the trouble. I will see to it that he gets something for his discomfort.'

He had returned to his brother's bedside unconvinced.

'I feel like a balloon,' Jack said. 'Feel the back of my neck.'

The flesh there was swollen and, when he touched the swelling, it had a distinctly spongy feeling. Most unpleasant.

'Good God. Like a punctured football bladder.'

'Thanks very much.'

'It will disappear, though, won't it?'

'So they say.'

An uncomfortable silence followed.

'You know I would sooner you didn't come.'

'What? Why do you say that?'

'It's so unfair. I look at you and you're fit and healthy and smell of the outdoors and I lie here knowing that I'm never coming out. It's so unfair. I don't deserve this.'

'Stop feeling sorry for yourself. Of course you'll come out.'

'Go to hell, George. Just go and don't come back.'

He had left the hospital thoroughly depressed and angry. He did return but they had never again spoken of that conversation.

Because of Jack he had studiously tried to avoid all contact with the disease and had found work with the Forestry Commission. The war had put an end to that commitment. He had been forced to mix with men from all parts of the country and his fastidious routines seemed so trivial in the circumstances.

Now of course advances in medicine have brought hope to the victims of TB. Streptomycin, in combination with other drugs, was driving down the death rate. Too late for Jack, though. Poor

Jack died of an infection. George blamed the pneumothorax for that and, from then on had distrusted the medical profession completely. Nevertheless, he is pleased with Glasgow's imaginative scheme.

'I hope it works,' he says.

'What?'

'The scheme, the project. Glasgow.'

'Scandalous waste of money if it doesn't.'

He wonders why she has become such a cynic. Perhaps their failure to have children.

'I must plant the seed potatoes this weekend.'

'A bit early surely.'

'Like to have them in by St Patrick's day.'

Poor Jack. He had always been the bookish member of the family, a frail indoor specimen who preferred public libraries to games pitches. It was Jack who had inspired his interest in wireless and telegraphy. He had built a crystal radio set through which he could hear faint voices and music with a set of earphones and, as he progressed to a more sophisticated set through which he could pick up short wave radio, Jack had passed the 'cat's whisker' on to him. He had taken it to boarding school and listened to it secretly in bed at night after 'lights out'. He had learnt Morse code so that he and Jack could communicate and together they built a transmitter and receiver so that they could speak to each other from room to room. Eventually they had built sets with which they could contact enthusiasts all over the country. They had joined the amateur radio network and, as radio 'hams' had their own call signs.

All that network was shut down when war was declared.

When their mother died shortly after Jack and the house was prepared for sale he had spent weeks dismantling the network of cables and aerials in the building. As he lifted the last receiver he found a notebook with Jack's last message written in his unmistakeably microscopic hand.

'Keep searching the airwaves. I will be out there somewhere. You just have to listen. Look after mother and cancel my sub to RSGB. We know I have a single ticket. Over and Out. Jack.'

All through the war he would find himself late at night twisting the knob on a receiver and gliding through the airwaves, wondering if at any minute he would hear Jack's voice or his call sign. It was like flying, imagining himself far out in dark space hoping to meet his brother, hoping that the journey from earth had cleansed him of his bitterness. He did not like remembering that conversation.

It was because of Jack that he had requested a posting to Signals when he enlisted.

'I should go and visit the cemetery,' he says, removing his pipe.

'Your mother's?'

'No. Jack.'

'What on earth brought that on?'

'I was thinking about him.'

'Morbid thought for a Saturday night, George. It's almost time for Saturday Night Theatre. You'd be better listening to that.'

'It was the talk of TB which reminded me. Perhaps I should get tested myself. Some of the houses I visit must be rife with it.'

'Don't be silly. You're as fit as a fiddle.'

'That doesn't prevent me contracting it. Yes, definitely, I will and you should too.'

'I will not! Just as likely to get it from the people in the queue. If I'm going to die, I'm going to die and that's that.'

'You might win an Austin.'

'So that's the real reason. I'm sent to a chest hospital and you get the car. Is that it?'

'Of course not.'

It did worry him, the thought of having TB but at least, if he had, the treatment was less barbaric. He hoped that, if he contacted the disease, he would not react like Jack, that he would face it with some dignity and courage. Still, he should have it checked.

Chapter 11

'Going up to George Square, Sligo?'

'Why? What's in George Square?'

'The X Ray thing. You must have heard.'

'Not me. I'm healthy. Look after myself.'

'You could win some fags.'

'Never won anything.'

'By the way, there was a guy asking for you.'

'For me?'

'Aye. O'Callaghan. That was it. Brian O'Callaghan. Said he was with you in Spain.'

'He's a liar then. Nobody by that name with me in Spain.'

There was, though, and I mind him fine. What does he want, eh? Fucken bastard. I walk away from the hostel warden so that he can't see my face.

O'Callaghan. Machine gunner. Said he'd been with the IRA before Spain but he didn't piss off like the other Paddies did when they found their NCO's had been with the Black and Tans. Funny that. Him shouting about the IRA yet taking orders from Black and Tan men. Saw him twice. 12th February on Suicide Hill above the Jarama River. I mind the smell of the thyme and the olive trees and the river shining in the sun. Some fucken Russian said we had to advance down the hill. Madness. Fascists were waiting for us. Nobody knew they'd crossed the river. Hundreds of them. Moroccans. Crack troops, heading straight for us. Mowing us down like ninepins. I can see them yet, dodging behind every rock and knoll. You couldn't get a crack at them.

'Fuck this for a game of soldiers,' I said and pulled back to the ridge. The others did too.

That's when I first saw O'Callaghan, kicking fuck out of his Maxim.

'What's wrong with you, you daft bastard?' I shouts. 'We need that thing.'

'Wrong ammo. Wrong fucken ammo.'

Russians. At least my rifle worked.

Then it started. Fascist shells screaming over and bursting among us, bodies and legs and hats flying in the air. Even the grass on the ridge was getting mowed down by the German machine guns. Condor Legion. Hell was too good a word for it. We were cut to pieces before we pulled back.

One good thing I mind. As we were leaving, the Moroccans reached the top of the hill just as O'Callaghan's boys got the right ammo and scythed them down like ripe corn. They ran like rabbits. We got back to the old farmhouse that night.

Next day this guy Springall comes in and says we've to attack and says there'll be aircraft and tanks to back us up. We headed back into hell. No tanks and three wee planes dropped a couple of bombs and fucked of. Didn't do much good. We were told to attack. 600 yards of open ground raked by machine guns. Our CO, Tam Wintringham, said no. Twice he said it. Brave man to ignore orders but he saved my life I reckon. Good man, Wintringham. A Commie and one of the few who knew what he was doing.

I go round to George Square an there's hundreds there, all queueing up for an X Ray. Like a holiday with flags an music. Maybe I should join them right enough. Do no harm. But what if I'm sick and have to go to one of those hospitals? Like they would send me. No choice. Have to give my name and address and that. Want to know all about you. No. Not for me.

I sit down on a bench and this woman looks at me as if I was a leper and gets up and walks away. Can't be that bad surely. I was at the baths last week. Anyway another woman comes over and sits. Fair worn out she looks with a face like a corpse and legs like spindles. You can see through the skin on her hands. Been pretty once.

'Here for the X Ray?' she says.

'No, no. Just resting.'

'I walked all the way frae Crown Street. Shoulda got a car.'

'You for an X Ray?'

'Aye. Think I know the result, though.'

'Not good, eh?'

'Spect they'll send me to one o they hospitals places outa town. Don't care much anyway. They took ma weans away – both o' them. Said I wisnae fit to look after them an that the single end was a squalor. That's what they said an I was doin ma best. Not much to live for really.'

'Don't say that, missus. You could get well and get the weans back so you could. Consumption's not the death sentence it used to be. Those new drugs work wonders. You could get well again.'

'Christ knows where the kids are now. Last I heard the boy was on a farm. Lassie could be anywhere. They send them abroad, you know, without tellin. Like they're not yours. Like they're their property. They don't care about us. The mothers.'

'Get well, missus, and start looking. Don't give up. Weans maybe living in hope that you'll find them. Maybe counting the days till you come.'

'Spose. Maybe I'll do that.'

I get up an head for the caff at the bridge.

'Thanks, mister,' she shouts behind me.

Half way across the square I mind about the boy on the railway He'd run away from a farm and was looking for his Ma.

I hurry back but she was gone and no sign of her in the queue.

I go round to the caff and get a mug of tea and a cheese roll. I'm sitting there quiet and fucken O'Callaghan comes over. Stinking of drink and filth. Old tweed overcoat humming with pee.

'Well Sligo. You haven't changed much. Uglier maybe an a face full o red biddy.'

'What do you want?'

'Nice way to greet a comrade. Didn't say I wanted anythin?'

'Well piss off then.'

'Like you did at Suicide Hill, eh?'

'What? What are you talking about?'

'You pissed off and left us to the fascists.'

'We obeyed orders.'

'Aye. That'll be right. You couldn't take it. Shower o cowards.'

'Overton's orders.'

'Aye an you left us up on the hill, hung out to dry, the whole company. Machine guns not much use when the fascists are right round you.'

'You surrendered.'

'That or die for Christ's sake.'

'Who was the coward, then? I'll tell you what happened. We regrouped and came back for you but the fascists turned the machine guns they'd taken off you on us. Your fucken guns. Cut us to ribbons. Six out of forty got back so don't give us that crap about cowards. Just fuck off and leave me in peace.'

'Oh I will, I will. But you listen first. There's a man in that hostel you're in called Doyle, Eamonn Doyle. An informer for the Brits. We lost dozens of good men cos of him. They say he still knows too much.'

'So?'

'It would be good if he met with an accident.'

'So?'

'You could arrange it.'

'Go to hell.'

'Thing is I could tell about the wine cellar.'

'What are you talking about?'

'The wine cellar behind Suicide Hill. Not mind that? Or too ashamed to remember?'

'Don't know what you're on about.'

'You and other yella bellies were found skulkin there an had to be driven back to the front at gun point.'

Christ. I mind it now. Young boys scared shitless, shivering in the cellar. Seen their pals cut to ribbons and couldn't face any more. Just wee boys, barely shaving.

'I was sent to get them. Went with Aitken. And they didn't need a gun. Aitken talked to them and they walked back. Four o them died.'

'That's your story. I heard you were one o the ones skulkin.'

'Believe what you want. Ask Jock Cunningham, he knows the truth. Why don't you just fuck off and leave me in peace, eh?'

'I haven't finished yet. I know about Liverpool Joe.'

'What about him?'

'That you killed him.'

I jump up and fling my tea in his face. A woman at the counter starts to come over.

'You bastard. You come near me again and I'll tear your fucken head off.'

I make for the door.

'It's all right, missus,' I says to her, 'I'm just going.'

'You were seen, boyo,' he shouts.

Polis'll believe anything. If he goes and says I killed Joe, they'll come looking for me. Sleekit bastard. Need to go, get to fuck out of here.

Chapter 12

'I think I've found Mick's mother.'

George subsides into his armchair and flattens out the evening paper on his knee. His wife turns down the volume on the wireless and prods the needles into her knitting.

'Good heavens. After all this time. How on earth did you find her?'

'The X Ray lists. I asked the girls to keep an eye out for her and there she was. At least I think it is her. Can't be many Bridget Crossans. She tested positive so she may be in one of the chest hospitals. I'm sure I'll be able to find her.'

'I'm sure you will but what's the point? You haven't found Mick, for heaven's sake. You've spent a great deal of time on that boy already.'

'Yes. I do feel responsible, though. My misjudgement. Should have seen through the Munros. Anyway his mother may know where he is.'

'Do you think she'll tell you? I doubt it.'

'I suppose you're right. Still, it's worth a try.'

George opens the newspaper, glances at the headline about Britain's Hydrogen bomb test in the Pacific, and turns to the crossword. He is vaguely aware of his wife passing him on her way to the kitchen. The familiar noises of a kettle filling, saucers rattling and a tea caddy opening are unconsciously comforting. A picture of the tea caddy with the young Queen flits through his mind. A car pulls in to a driveway in the street outside. That'll be Mr Menzies with his new Austin no doubt. He imagines the car gleaming beside the Menzies bungalow, one of a row of bungalows in the quiet avenue all built in the years before the war. A peaceful enclave, a haven, virtually untouched by the convulsions of conflict. All the men in 'reserved occupations'. There are times when their modest prosperity and immunity from hardship annoys him, their three-piece suits and trilby hats. Yet he barely knows them. He keeps himself to himself.

When Violet comes through with the tea tray and lays it on the small table between their chairs he sees that he has not looked at the crossword.

'I have to go to Tiree next week,' he announces.

'Not again.'

She lifts her hand-knitted tea cosy off the teapot and gives the tea another stir.

'It's three months since I visited. Before that almost a year. I just can't get round all the placements. Far too many children boarded out and far too few inspectors to visit. No wonder there are cases of cruelty and neglect.'

'Better than their lives in the city, George. You said that yourself.'

'Not always true, though. Look at Mick. It's the assumptions behind it all that annoys me – the view that the city children must be saved from a mire of immorality, filth, poverty and sickness and sent to a healthy, God-fearing, loving family home in the Highlands. Little credence given to the valiant city mothers who toil tirelessly in the face of insurmountable hardship to keep their children. Too many middle class officials making harsh judgements about conditions and whisking the children away without a thought.'

'You're one of those yourself. Middle class.'

'Thank you very much. I think I have more insight into the struggles of these people than most or at least more sympathy. I can think of cases where the child being "in moral danger" was nothing more than a failure to attend mass.'

'On the whole, though, it must be better to place them in the countryside. Generally speaking I mean.'

She pours milk in the teacups – always milk first – and then tips in the tea. George takes a half spoon of sugar and dips his ginger biscuit in the tea.

'I wish you wouldn't do that,' she says.

'I'm not saying that there aren't successes. Last summer I visited a croft on Tiree and found the children – brother and sister – not only cared for but really happy. Certainly it was glorious weather which probably affected the whole family. They were shearing the sheep at the time, the men on clipping stools with their backs to

the dyke, the foster father among them as jovial as Harry
Secombe. The boy was hauling out the sheep to be clipped and
the girl was carrying fleeces for the grandfather to roll and
smearing tar on any cuts on the ewes. All working together. When
the mother brought out tea to the fank the children sat beside her
and you could see the affection between them. Not all like that
on the island certainly. Not by any means but that was one lot
which seemed to be a success.'

'The hedge needs cut again.'

'What ?'

'The hedge needs cut.'

He thinks of the vintage hedge shears which he had bought at
a displenishing sale but also his Raleigh bike and the ride he had
planned by the river. His neighbours' hedges are all meticulously
groomed and their lawn edges clipped. He cannot muster any
enthusiasm for such tidiness. He does enjoy growing vegetables.
There is some point in that. He returns to the crossword.

As he walks up the long avenue of buildings in the hospital
grounds, he remembers his brother's suffering. Today, however,
the trees are in blossom and the grounds echo with the thud of
a football and the shouts of men on the pitch. It is hard to be
gloomy.

He finds the woman in a bed on a veranda under a glass roof.
The row of beds has little space between each one so he remains
at the foot. Her dark hair, freshly washed, hangs limply round her
face. She does not smile and her eyes study him with hostility.

'Bridget Crossan?'

'Who are you?'

'George Buchanan, I'm a Children's Officer.'

'One o them, are you?'

'Do you have a son called Michael?'

'If I have weans, your crowd took them away long ago.'

'I was not involved in that and I don't approve of taking
children from their parents unless it is absolutely necessary. I was
asked to find a placement with foster parents for a boy called Mick
Crossan and I managed to place him with a couple on a farm.
Since then he has been missing for some time and I'm really

worried about him. Could this be your son? He has red hair and a scar on his left eyebrow.'

'If he's ma son, he'll be fine, he'll survive.'

'Yes. The Mick I know is an intelligent, able boy. The couple on the farm were not good to him. My misjudgement, I'm afraid. So he left of his own accord.'

'So he's done a runner, eh? Good for him.'

'Yes. He was quite right but I still worry about him.'

'He'll be lookin for me. He won't know I'm here.'

'So he is your Mick?'

'Aye. Can you tell him I'm here.?'

'If I could find him.'

'They took ma girl too, you know. I tried to find where she was, tried to get her back but they wouldn't tell me nothin, nothin. One of her pals said they'd sent her to Canada but they wouldn't tell me. Don't spose I'll ever see her again. I could have got them back too. I got a good job cleanin in a big house. Six days an good pay. They wouldn't listen.'

He longs to offer to find the girl but that would be exceeding his remit. The Committee were determined to keep their children and the parents apart. Such contact created a risk of their wards sliding back into their old immoral ways. Yet he feels sorry for Bridget and decides to make an effort to find her daughter.

'I'm sorry. What was your daughter's name?'

'Maeve. I want to see Mick.'

'I will do everything I can to find him, I promise you that.'

'He's a good boy. He used to help me all he could.'

'He was good on the farm and I think he liked the work. Is his father still alive?'

'No, no. He was killed. Got crushed against a wall by a lorry. Tore off his arm an crushed his chest. They said it was his fault. Shouldn't have been there. Left me wi the weans. I did ma best, mister.'

'I'm sure you did.'

'We wis okay when he was alive. Always had money. He wasn't bad that way. Worked down at Dalbeattie on the bomb factory an then knockin down air-raid shelters around the city. Good money. When he died I had to knock ma pan in to feed the weans.

Now I'm stuck here.'

'Maybe the rest will do you good, the rest and decent food.'

'Food might be fine if I could taste it. Everythin tastes o the medicine. PAS they ca it. Disgustin. Twelve wee rice paper sachets three times a day an Strep jags twice a day in ma hip. Fair baggit I am.'

'Better than it used to be. At least the medication works. At least you have a future.'

'Aye maybe. God knows when I'll get outa here.'

'Is there anything I can get you? I will come back and keep you informed.'

'Get me Mick. That would be ma best medicine. You could get us some oranges or apples, if you like. I don't like askin but they're ma favourites.'

'Of course. I'll do what I can.'

As he walks away towards the main gate he resolves to trace her daughter. If he finds her, he will decide then whether to tell her. No harm in searching in the meantime. As for Mick, he wonders what he will do when he finds him. Clearly it will be some time before he can be returned to his mother. It will have to be another placement. This time, however, he will be especially careful. Perhaps he should start looking in advance, prepare the way, identify and reserve a place for Mick. Against the rules but who is to know?

Chapter 13
MICK

'That priest's been here again lookin for you.'

'Nosey bastard.'

I stands outside her door in the close. She's shiverin though it's no a cold day. Sun was shinin when I was out wi the milk. Spose it's cold in the close right enough an her dress is awfu thin.

'Mary,' her Ma calls from inside. 'Are ye no away yet?'

'Aye, Ma. Just goin. I've to go to the shop for a loaf, Mick. Are you comin?'

'Aye, right.'

She skips down the stair an I come after but no skippin.

'Where've you been stayin, Mick?'

'That would be tellin.'

'Come on. You can tell me. Am I no yer best pal?'

I like the way her hair swings as she skips. Is she ma best pal? Trust nobody, that's what Davey said. Maybe he was right. But I'd like to tell her. A wee secret between us. Just her an me.

'Aye, you are.'

'Well then.'

Someone has pee'd in the close. Dirty bastard. We steps round it an out into the street.

'Sleep in the hay loft in the stable.'

'Jesus. Are you no frozen?'

'Na. It's warm. Even in winter.'

'All this time you've been there.'

'Aye.'

'Ma was always askin where you were stayin.'

'Just as well you didn't know, eh?'

'What's the milkman say? Does he know?'

'He does now. He comes in one mornin last back end an I'd slept in an he caught me.

"What the fuck are you doing up there?" he shouts. Fair beelin' he was an I says, "I came in earlier an fell asleep, mister. I'm really

74

sorry." "You're a fucken liar, you wee bastard" he says. So I comes down an be's all humble like and tells him I've no home to go to an please, please can I stay an he says, "I knew you was a liar, you wee shite. How long have you been sleeping up there?" "Just a week" but I'd been there for months. "All right," he says, "but I know nothing about it. If anyone finds out, you broke in, right? An if I catch you smokin, I'll cut your fucken throat and tip you in the river."

'So he let you stay?'

'Aye. He knows I look after the horse an he says I'm the best worker he's had. I chat up the customers an have all the patter.'

'Real charmer, eh?'

I takes I her hand. I don't know why. I just did it like.

'What are you doin?' she says but doesn't pull it away.

'Do you mind?'

'Think you're my boyfriend or somethin?'

'Why not?'

'You stay away all these months an never say nothin an me an ma Ma wonderin what's happened an you think you can just waltz back in an be ma boyfriend?'

'I was scared o that priest, scared he would tell.'

'Tell what?'

Trust no-one, Davey said, but I look at her an want to tell her, want to give her somethin.

'I've no Da. I was boarded out an sent to a farm an they battered me stupid an I ran away an came to look for my Ma.'

'Jesus, Mick, that's awfu.'

She squeezes ma hand an I go warm inside an I'm glad I telt her.

'Did you no find yer Ma then?'

'Na. I keep lookin though.'

'I hope you find her.'

We go past a coal lorry an wait for a man wi a leather jacket carryin a sack o coal into a close. His face is all black an his mouth looks all red. When he's in the close I lets go her hand an leans over the lorry deck an grabs some bitsa coal into ma pockets.

'For your Ma.'

'Bloody thief,' she laughs.

I takes her hand again an we go past the bookie's place an this man comes out. Moustache an hair oil an smart jacket.

'Well, Mary,' he says sorta flirtin like, 'this your boy friend?'

'Kinda.'

'What's your name, son?'

'Robert.'

'Robert is it? No Bob or Bobby or Rab. All hoity-toity. Robert what?'

'O'Donnell.'

'He's ma cousin,' says Mary.

'Is he now? You can't marry your cousin. Did you know that?'

'He's ma second cousin.'

'Or fourth or fifth, eh? You're not a good liar, Mary. I've seen you on the milk cart, Sir Robert, an your boss speaks very highly of you. How about working for me – part time like?'

'Doin what?'

'A runner. You look like an honest boy.'

'A bookie's runner?'

'Aye.'

'That'd be great.'

'Come round here tomorrow back of two an come to the door. I'll make a man of him for you, Mary. See you later, alligators.'

He swanks off. Crepe-sole shoes an red socks. I'm not sure about it. Polis raid these places whiles an I might get caught. Bookies pay the fines o the punters but maybe not runners. Anyway, don't want the polis askin questions.

'You goin to go?' she says.

'Aye. It's good money.'

'Maybe, but I know a boy got his face slashed. Punter said the boy lost a winnin line.'

'I can run. Fancy a walk to the milk yard? I could show you where I sleep.'

'Ma feet are killin me in these shoes.'

'I'll buy you new shoes.'

'Don't be daft.'

'I will. I promise.'

'Anyway I've to get back.'

'Aye. Right enough. Better get the bread.'

We gets back to her close an we stops in the street.

'Gonna give us a kiss?' I says.

'If you give us fag.'

I'm getting ma woodbine out an I sees the bloody priest comin down the stair behind her.

'Shit! Gotta go.'

An I runs like a rabbit.

'I'll be back,' I shouts.

She stands there frownin wi her mouth open.

Don't know if the bastard saw me.

Chapter 14

Bridget, named after St Brigid of Kildare, is not a saint. Yet she has lain with no other man since her husband died. All her energy had been consumed by the endless struggle to provide for her children, a struggle which had slowly but inexorably worn away her strength.

Now she lies in her bed in the open air under a glass canopy, looking at her hands. Her nails, once chipped and cracked, have grown and her fingers, once calloused and pitted with soot, are clean and smooth. The hands of a lady she thinks. She is propped up on pillows unlike the women on either side who lie flat and have fallen asleep.

Her face is too long to be beautiful yet, with her striking blue eyes under crow black hair, men tend to notice her. It is said that ships from the Spanish Armada were wrecked off the west coast of Ireland and that some survivors mingled with the Irish leaving progeny of exceptional Spanish beauty. Her neighbours were convinced that she had Spanish blood, a conviction which infuriated her father.

She looks up as a man coughs on the path below her veranda. Tall, gaunt, with a tweed cap and sports jacket, he carries the air of the countryside in spite of his pallor.

'I'm sorry. Did I wake you?' he says.

'No. I wasn't asleep.'

'My first day out. They've allowed me out for a walk.'

'I wish I could do that.'

'I'm sure you will one day. Just need patience.'

'I'm no good at that.'

He laughs and she likes the way his eyes laugh too.

'Have you been here long?'

'Since last year. Too long. I hate lyin about.'

'I'm sure. You from the city?'

'Aye. South side.'

'Don't know that part. In fact I've hardly ever been in the city. I've a farm in the country, in Lanarkshire. On the Lang Whang.'

'Bet you miss that, eh?'

'Yes. Bad time to be away as well with the lambing. Have to pay a man to see to it. Eighty pounds.'

'My God! A lot o money.'

'No choice I'm afraid. Can't leave them to lamb themselves.'

A silence moves between them.

'Better get on my way. Get some strength back in my legs. Can I get you anything?'

'No. I'm fine thanks.'

'My name's Mathew by the way. Hope you'll be up and about soon.'

'So do I. I'm Bridget.'

'Nice to meet you. Perhaps we'll meet again.'

He touches the peak of his cap and moves on. Nice man. She watches him as he walks away. Upright like a soldier. It is easy to imagine him striding across the fields with a dog at his heels. A farmer like her father, though you could hardly describe those miserable patches of land with which he had fought all his life as a farm. He had never walked upright like Mathew but had a permanent stoop as if he carried a sack of potatoes on his shoulders. Strong, though. He could lift a young stirk on to his back. She remembers him cutting turf out on the bog, his sleaghan slicing easily and rhythmically through the black turf. She had brought him buttermilk and fresh soda bread for lunch. Long ago. He is buried in the graveyard facing the Atlantic.

She would like to be buried there too. Certainly not in Glasgow. She had been forced to think about it when they told her she had TB. Terrified at first, believing it was a death sentence, but the doctor had explained that the new drugs provided a cure. Yet she knew of people who died in spite of the medication, so was not reassured. She had gone home and launched herself into a fierce task of scrubbing and washing to keep the fear at bay, to drive it to the back of her mind. It lurked there, waiting to surface as soon as she stopped to think. It rushed out and shook her like a dog with a rat. She had hurried to the hospital to escape it, forgetting that people would die there too, one in a bed beside her.

She wonders if Connor would have visited her. He hated doctors and had stayed away from the house when the children were born. One of the midwives thought she was a single mother and had told her how to have the baby adopted. Shocked by the suggestion, she had made sure that Connor was introduced for the next birth. Of course there were times when she had been tempted to abandon the children but Connor's death induced a fierce determination to keep them. Had he lived, they would never have been taken away. She imagines him standing at the end of her bed, his overalls slimy with grease, his cap tilted, his piece bag slung across his shoulder and his fag cupped in his fist. Swaying awkwardly from boot to boot, he frowns and clearly longs to leave. She smiles. The truth is he would never have come.

Ah, Connor the charmer. The boy with the lightning feet and strong arms that could lift her off her feet on the dance floor. The flash teenager with the American airforce bomber jacket, the Philip Morris fags and the Zippo lighter with the pin-up girl on the front. They met at the Locarno in Sauchiehall Street after the war. She was surprised and flattered by his attention and astonished to find that they had crossed from Ireland on the same boat, he from Sligo and she with her father from Donegal. Her father had been furious when he heard of the liaison, returning from the hydro scheme in the north to scold her for going out with a Prod, but, as always, she had won him over.

'Have they been round with the pills?' croaks the woman in the next bed.

'No. Not yet.'

'Bloody freezing isn't it?'

'Aye.'

'Who's the man you were talking to?'

'Don't know. I thought you were asleep.'

'Is he the one that brought the oranges?'

'No.'

'More than one admirer then?'

'He's a Childrens' Officer that one. Tryin to find my son.'

'Take him off you, did they?'

'Aye. And ma girl.'

'Because you were sick?'

'No. Before that. Cos they said I couldn't manage.'

'Awful to lose a child. I lost two sons in the war, one in a convoy to Russia and one in Burma. No-one talks about Burma of course – the forgotten war.'

'I'm sorry. At least mine's alive – I think.'

'I hope they find him.'

'But, if they do, they'll just put him in a home 'cos I'm in here. Hellish places. Slap them, beat them, put them in cold baths, kick the livin daylights out o them. Aye, an dirty things too done to them.'

'Surely not. These places are inspected and the staff are good Christian, compassionate people, professionals. I think your children are making things up to win your sympathy.'

'One thing about my children. They don't lie.'

'Nonsense. All children tell fibs at some point. If you think it's true, you should tell the authorities.'

'An they would believe me? Don't be daft. They're all in it together. If you say anythin, they just haul the wagons into a circle like they do in the movies an turn the guns on you. They don't listen to the likes of us. Deny everythin. I don't want Mick goin to a home. In a way I hope he stays on the run. Not safe but better than they places.'

Twin scarlet blotches flame on her cheeks and her jaw thrusts forward. The woman is on the other side and has a plummy voice. More like some she has cleaned for in the houses with gardens. Yet she's sorry for her too. Must be hard losing two sons in the war. Maybe they were all she had. The war had barely touched her village in Donegal. She had seen seaplanes flying over the bay and watched an armed trawler tow one of them to Bundoran.

Her father spat when he saw it. "Bloody British. In our country" he said. The boat was based in Killybegs and he had warned her never to speak to the sailors in the village Yet, with several other men, he had climbed Fintragh to rescue the crew of a British bomber which crashed on the mountain near the end of the war. The crew were killed but he helped to carry the bodies down the hill. "Some mothers' sons," he said.

She misses him, his tortured English, his inverted smile, his cheek with the black hair above the razor line. Those were good days, the days at home on the croft. The warm flank of the cow on her brow at the milking, the sweet scent of meadow grass behind her father's scythe, the glow of the oil lamp in the kitchen at night and his stocking feet stretched out in front of the fire. She should have stayed there with her mother after he left for Scotland. She would never have got sick in the clean air of Donegal.

'Good afternoon, Bridget.'
 'Hello. Sorry, I was half asleep.'
 'Better today ?'
 'I don't know. One day is the same as the next. I s'pose I'm better than when I came.'
 Mathew. That's his name. She should have remembered.
 'Well, that's good. You're looking better.'
 'Warmer today. Good for the lambs.'
 'Yes indeed. You know about sheep.'
 'My Daddy had sheep – a score of them. I used to help with the lambs, take them to the fire when they were foundered, feed them when they were weak.'
 'Could do with you on my place. I'm just myself and have to do all that.'
 'Maybe you give me a job when I'm better.'
 'Now that's a great idea. Can you shear as well?'
 'Aye. Used to shear for our neighbours too.'
 'Excellent. Not many lady shepherds around but I don't see why. I'm sure they'll be just as good as a man. Tell you what. You get better and I'll take you on. A bargain?'
 He steps up on to the veranda beside her bed and holds out his hand.
 'A bargain.'
 She shakes his hand, noticing the calloused knuckles.
 He steps back down.
 'I mean it,' he says and smiles before walking away.
 She twirls one of her dark locks in her fingers.

Chapter 15
MICK

I goes round to the shop but the door's shut an I can't look in 'cos the window's all boarded up. Sign above the door says 'grocers' but it's old an scabby. Paint's peelin off. I take out a packet and light a fag. Wonder if I should knock. This man comes hurryin down the street. No bonnet on but face all black to the bonnet line an white above it. Sweatin an wheezin.

'Did he get my line?' he says.

'What?'

'Francis. Did he get my line?'

'I don't know.'

'For Christ's sake, son. Is he in?'

'I don't know.'

'Jesus Christ!'

He batters on the door.

'Francis! Are you there? You are. I know you're in there. Open the fucken door, Francis.'

The door opens and the swank wi the brothel creepers peers out.

'For God's sake, Tam. Do you want to bring the polis on us?'

'Did you get my line?'

'Of course I got it. Come inside.'

He sees me.

'What are you doin here?'

'You told me to come an you'd give me a job.'

'Did I? Oh aye, you're Mary's pal. You come in too.'

Inside the place is a shambles. A blackboard like school with figures chalked on it. Huners o paper slips an newspapers on a table an all over the floor. A wireless shoutin in the corner about a horse race.

'You got my slip?' the man says.

'Aye, aye. Hold your wheest for God's sake. Was it each way or on the nose?'

Francis, if that's his name, rummages through the slips on the table.

'Straight on. What were the odds?'

'Six to one.'

'Ya beauty! Good old Pride of Glenree. Not for the knackers yet.'

Francis looks none too pleased but pulls a wad o notes from his pocket an pays the man.

'Good for you, Frankie boy! Mind and send a boy tomorrow. I'm off to celebrate.'

'Shut the door after you.'

He bangs it as he goes. Francis rolls up the wad an sticks it back in his pocket.

'What's your name, son? I can't mind.'

'Robert.'

'Oh aye. That's right. If you're gonna work for me, you'll need to get to know every street and every close around my patch.'

'I will. I know some o them already.'

'Here's the drill, well. See that satchel there. You take that and go to where I tell you. Punter'll give you a slip with cash wrapped in it. It goes in the satchel. Then you go to the next place and get another but see each one goes in carefully. They mustn't get mixed. I don't want to have to sort them out before the race. If any go missing, the punter'll come after you and slice open your pretty face. Spoil your whole day, son. Have you got that?'

'Aye.'

'You'll get a cut of the week's takings every Saturday night.'

'Great stuff.'

We stop an look in the shop window. Mary has white socks on specially.

'Do you see any you like?' I says.

'That red pair. Real classy.'

'Could you walk on them?'

I have a picture of her staggerin down the street like a drunk an her Ma yellin that she's a slut.

'Keep them for the dancin and that.'

We goes into the shop an the shop lady comes over lookin like we'd shat ourselves.

'Can I help you?'

'The red shoes in the window,' I says. 'Can she try them on?'

'What size is she? What size are you dear?'

'I don't know.'

'You don't know? Well, sit down and we'll measure.'

Mary sits and the shop lady pulls up a stool an a measurin thing an takes off Mary's sandal. Her white sock has a hole in the toe.

'We don't have that shoe in your size, dear. It's a lady's fashion shoe. Maybe you could choose something else, something more suitable for younger women. There's a range of teenage shoes over there. Have a look.'

Mary hobbles over an I go an stand beside her.

'Don't like any o this lot, Mick. I want the red ones.'

She looks like she's goin to greet so I says,

'Get the red ones then. Get the size nearest.'

We goes back to the shop lady,

'I want to try on the red one. The nearest my size.'

The woman whistles down her nose an gets a box off the shelf an slides one on to Mary's foot.

'Much too large, I'm afraid, but it does look good on you. Try a few steps.'

Mary tries to walk but it keeps slipping off.

'Perhaps if you wore thick socks.'

'I want these ones. They're real classy.'

'Very good, dear. Take it off and I'll wrap them up. That'll be two pounds five shillings.'

I takes out my cash but there isn't enough.

'Can you keep them for us missus? I'll have to get to the bank.'

'Oh. I see. I'll keep them till tomorrow at closing time. No longer.'

'Thanks missus. I'll be back. I will.'

We goes out an Mary's not pleased.

'Black affronted. Thought you had enough.'

'So did I. Come tomorrow same time an we'll get them.'

'Don't know if I will. So embarrassed. I'm away home.'

She marches away, her hands in wee fists.

I still feel bad about yesterday. I hope she'll come today. I got a sub off the milkman so I've enough now but I'll have to lay off the fags so I will. I goes down to the bookie's place after the milk round. Two other runners there just leavin.

'You're late, pal,' one says, 'Frankie's beilin.'

I goes in an Frankie's countin cash.

'About bloody time, you wee bastard. Here's your list. There's two new ones in Gorbals Street. You'll need to run like fuck. First race is in an hour.'

I grabs the satchel and runs like a rabbit.

Half way round an I'm pechin like a pig an I've to meet Mary. Christ, I'll never make it. Can't stop or I'll get my throat cut. What the fuck'll I do? If I don't meet her, she'll dump me, sure as God. I know. I'll take a risk. Long way to the shop. Run. Run like...Satchel's flappin on ma arse. Polis over the street lookin at me. Hope he doesn't run too.

Crash through girls playin peever. Wee dog snappin at ma heels. Try to kick it an near fall over. Chest's burnin but keep goin.

She's there.

Stop beside her an near puke.

Dig in ma pocket an pull out the cash.

'Here. You get them. Can't stop.'

'But Mick...'

'Gotta go.'

An I takes off again.

I made it back in time. I throws the satchel on the desk.

'Jesus,' Frankie says, 'You're in some state. Sweat's lashing off you. You get them all?'

'Aye.'

'Good lad. Better sit down.'

'No. Need to go.'

'Come back after. Think I'll have a wee bonus for you.'

I goes back to the shop but there's no sign of Mary. Shit.

'Did ma sister get the shoes?' I ask the shop lady.

'Yes. She's delighted with them. They're twenty sizes too big but she's as happy as Larry.'

'Thanks, missus.'

I'm dying for a fag but I'm skint. Better go back to Frankie.

Door's shut but I hear the wireless inside so I knock.

'Who's that?'

'Robert.'

He opens the door an lets me in.

He's busy countin cash – a lot of it.

'Lucky day. Made a killin today. Won't be a minute.'

He goes back to countin.

There's a knock at the door an a man shouts, 'Frankie are you in there?'

Frankie puts his finger to his mouth an says shush.

The man kicks in the door. Not a big man but face like one o they bulldogs snarlin an slaverin.

'Where's ma winnin's Frankie?'

'What winnings, Jazz? What are you talking about? Your brother-in-law lifted your money for you half an hour ago.'

'I don't have a brother-in-law, Frankie boy.'

Frankie looks awful scared.

'I swear to you this man came in, gave me your pen-name, said he was your brother-in-law and I gave him your winnings.'

'You're a rotten liar, Frankie.'

The man leans over an lifts Frankie by the collar an flings him against the wall. Frankie makes a queer noise like a burst bag an tries to breathe. The man goes over an smashes him in the face an then goes to the table an lifts a wad o notes an walks out. Blood's drippin off Frankie's chin. Face looks like a dog chewed it. Eyes shut. Maybe he's dead. Christ, Mick, it's time to go. Anyone comes in they'll think you did it. Get to fuck out of it. Grab a wad o notes on the way. He won't know.

But no. That's not right. Ma would say that's wrong. She wouldn't scarper an leave a man in that state.

I goes over to Frankie an kneels beside him.

'You okay, Frankie?'

He shakes his head an says somethin but I can't make it out.

'What did you say, Frankie?'

'Get Maggie.'

'Who's Maggie?'

'Thistle Street. Nineteen. Top right. Go.'

I goes out an bangs the door shut an runs like fuck.

Chapter 16
SLIGO

Here somewhere. Hut's the same but the bank's covered in that bomb-site plant and its seed's blowin everywhere like dandelion clocks. I'll go back on to the rail track and look again. There. Just there by that bush. Scramble up the bank and dig. Shovel without a shaft but better than bare hands. Fucken roots weren't here when I buried it. Dig deeper. Must be here but I'm near down to the rock. Got to find it. Be ready for O'Sullivan. Bit to the left, Sligo.

Here she is! Tin's rusty but the lid opens no bother. Oil cloth's good as new. Unwind it and there she is. You beauty! Not a mark on her. Good as new. Luger and ammo case. Feels good in the hand and the ammo slides in with a click. I mind when I got it. Fascist officer I shot in the back of the head near Suicide Hill. They were retreating and, after they'd all gone, I went out to look at him. Didn't go out for booty or anything. Just to look at him. See the man I killed. Rolled him over to see his face but there wasn't much left to see. I didn't feel nothing. Seen men kick and swear at bodies they'd killed. Wasn't like that. Just felt nothing. Just thought it could have been me lying there. Spotted the holster and took the gun.

Knew it would be safe here on the West Highland Line. Now head north away from the city. O'Sullivan and his pals won't find me there. Got the Luger in case.

***

Lookin down on Tyndrum. Some view across the glen over to the mountains. Still a wee patch of snow near the top o that one though it's summer. You can see the other rail line down below, the one goin to Oban. The one up here goes to Fort William.

Half-asleep last night in the hut I hear footsteps on the track outside. I lie still and click the ammo into the Luger. Steps keep comin but stop outside the hut. I stop breathin.

Just one o them I reckon. He puts his head in the door. I can just see him.

'Stay where you are,' I says.

'Mother of God!'

'Fuck off and keep walkin.'

'Sorry, mister. I just wanted a lie down.'

'Keep goin, well. There's another hut further up.'

'Please, mister. I can't go another step. Been walkin since dawn and the midges out here are fierce.'

'Stay where you are.'

I blow up the embers till there's a flame so's I can see him. Just young wi a donkey jacket and hair sproutin from his skull like heather. A bit scared.

'Sit over there.'

He sits with his back to the wall. There's a hole in the sole of his boot.

'Where are you headin, son ?'

'Oban.'

'God's sake. You're on the wrong line.'

'What? The walker in Stirling said just follow the line through Callander and up by Balquhidder and Crianlarich.'

'Line forks at Crianlarich.'

'He never said.'

'I'll show you in the mornin.'

'Where are going, mister?'

'Never mind that.'

'I'm goin to Mull. My brother's cuttin bracken there. Good money he says.'

'Why are you walkin then, eh?'

'My Mam gave me money and I drank it all in Glasgow.'

'That was clever. I'm sure she'd be proud of you. You could have hitched a lift.'

'Brother said not to. Said no lifts. Drivers stop in the middle of nowhere and steal your money.'

'That's bollocks. Anyway, get some sleep and I'll show you the Oban line in the mornin.'

In the daylight I can see he's just a boy with hair like copper wire. Sound asleep.

I blow up the fire and hangs the tea can over the flame.

Never been to Mull. Might be a good place to go to get away. Don't know about buroo money, though. Should get back to Glasgow for that. Maybe you can get it out there. Big place. I think it is anyway. Must be an office there surely.

Can's boilin. Shake the tea in. Swirls round on the water. Look round and he's starin at me.

'You slept then.'

'Yes, mister. Till that bloody train came. What a racket. Jesus, I thought it was comin over the top of us.'

'There'll be another any time.'

'I'll know what it is this time. I'm starvin. Is it far to Oban?'

'Have you any money?'

He looks at me as if I was goin to steal it.

'No. I told you.'

'Well here. Here's half a crown. You go down to the village and get some bread and cheese. Leave your donkey jacket.'

'Eh?'

'In case you think about not comin back. A bit of insurance. Not that it's worth much.'

'Why don't you go?'

'Never mind that. If you're starvin, go. Down to the main road turn right.'

The boy tosses his jacket in the corner and leaves.

Mull. Aye maybe. Says there's good money in it but I don't know if I could wield a scythe any more. Doubt it. No, definitely not. Roll a fag and wait for the boy.

Can hear the train chuggin up from Crianlarich. That'll be the sleeper likely. I'll look out and maybe the stoker'll throw off some coal. They're good that way.

Train passes and there you are. What did I say? A shovel of coal by the track.

I go to pick it up and see the boy comin back.

'Are you Sligo?' he says.

'No. Why?'

'Man at the shop has a message for a man called Sligo.'

'What man?'

'The shop man.'

'For Christ's sake! The owner do you mean?'

'Aye. The shop man. He has a message for a man called Sligo.'

'Whoever he is. Did you get the stuff?'

He hands me the bag and some change.

'You're honest anyway.'

We sit in the hut and eat the bread and cheese with a can o tea.

'You said you'd show me the way to Oban.'

'So I will. When I'm ready.'

I roll another fag and lean against the wall. Better douse the fire. A message for me? For Sligo? No-one knows I'm here. Not even O'Sullivan. I've told no-one I walk the lines.

'Right, son. Let's go.'

We walk to the station and down the hill over to the other line. Maybe go with him to Oban. Not a bad place. You can get fish for nothin' off the boats when the seine netters are in. Fresh silver herrin. Aye and there's a cave there you can doss in.

'I'll come with you.'

'What for?'

'Never mind what for. Just walk,eh? Not on the sleepers, you bampot.'

Chapter 17

'They've found Mick!'

George flings his hat towards the hatstand in the hall and is rewarded by a direct hit on the peg. He shakes off his coat and marches through to the sitting room. His wife glances up from her knitting but doesn't allow his enthusiasm to interrupt her clicking needles.

'For heaven's sake sit down, George. You're far too excited.'

'I am. I am. I'm so pleased.'

He obeys but sits on the edge of his chair.

'He was working as a bookie's runner and, when the police raided the shop, they caught him. His mother will be so pleased.'

'They are dreadful, these people, employing children. Bit like Fagin. Bad enough taking money from those who can least afford it but to exploit children as well is appalling.'

'I know. I suppose it is better than seeing them starve or stealing.'

'I've heard that the police turn a blind eye to it all, even pay the fines when the bookies end up in court. Pernicious habit gambling. The ruin of many poor families.'

'Indeed. Dreadful. The good thing is I've heard of a farm which might suit Mick perfectly. They seem to be good, hard-working people.'

'I suppose that means another farm visit in some remote part of the Highlands.'

'I'm afraid it does.'

'Well, don't forget the church fête.'

'Of course not. I'll arrange it round that. First, though, I must inform his mother.'

'I hate you visiting that place, I'm sure you carry TB back with you.'

'Nonsense, dear.'

***

'I have good news for you, Bridget.'

She is looking better today, more alert, more lively. We meet in the day room. She is taller than I thought and, in spite of the skeletal frame, there is a strength in the way she holds herself.

'You've found Mick!'

'Yes indeed.'

'Is he all right ? Can I see him?'

'He's fine. Unfortunately he is being held in care at the moment until I find him a placement on a farm.'

'I can't see him then?'

'Not at the moment.'

He is tempted to arrange a visit but dare not proceed. The Committee would take a dim view of such a contravention of policy. Callous really but that's how it is.

'Where was he?'

'The police raided a bookie's premises and found him there. They don't know where he was living and he won't say. I expect he has been looking for you.'

'Aye. They should never have took him away.'

'I'm sure you're right. It wasn't my decision.'

'You all say that. When you see him, tell him I love him, will you?'

'Of course.'

'What about Maeve?'

'I'm sorry I've not had time to search the files for her. I know which home she was taken to but I'll have to examine their files to locate her and, even then, it may be difficult.'

'You promised.'

'And I will try. The main thing at the moment is that Mick is safe and well.'

'Aye. I wish I could see him, though.'

'I'm sure. Is there anything I can get you?'

'Get me out o here. No, thanks. There's a gentleman here gets me things now and again. Anyway, they say I'll get home soon.'

'That's splendid. The same address?'

'God knows. After all this time in here they've probably let the house to someone else but Mathew, the man who brings me things, says I can have a job with him and there's a bothy there so maybe I'll be all right.'

'But how will I find you?'

She rummages in her pocket and produces a crumpled piece of paper.

'Here. That's Mathew's address. If I'm not there, God knows where I'll be.'

He copies the address into his notebook and hands back the paper.

'Many thanks. I'll be off then. I'll let you know about Mick.'

As he walks away he replaces his tweed hat and tugs at the brim.

***

Dear Mr Phillips,

I thought I would take some time to give you my impression of the farm before I complete my formal report as I thought it might help you to envisage the environment in which I hope to place Mick. Poor boy he deserves some kindness after the cruelty he experienced in the last place. I don't think I have ever seen a child in such a state, cowering and trembling in a dark corner in a pool of urine. I hope that these people will help to heal the psychological wounds inflicted by the Munros.

I arrived on the island yesterday, found accommodation in a guest house and visited the farm. I did see the place on a fine day certainly. Set on a steep south-facing slope in a wide valley, the farm buildings seem to cling to the hillside with a tenacity typical of island townships. The road leading down to the shore and the small village runs along the rough grazing above the farm, probably to avoid the marshland down by the river. The track down to the buildings is so steep that one has to take care not to slip but the view from the top is spectacular. As the bus drove away I stood for a while enjoying the tranquillity, a stillness broken only by the honking of the wild geese overhead. Beneath me a thin column of smoke curled into the crisp air from the farmhouse, a smart white building attached to the byre and piggery. The pungent smell of pigs strikes the senses like a hammer blow as one descends towards the yard.

No-one came to greet me so I had some time to take note of the buildings grouped round the yard. On the left there is an old farm cottage in which, as it turned out, Mick was to be housed. A modest stone building with two stories erected perhaps at the turn of the century, its windows and door face directly into the yard. Beyond it, a long barn stowed with baled hay and a milling shed with a bruising machine for oats. On the right the two-storey traditional farmhouse sits with its back to the yard – there may be a small garden at the front but it was hidden from view. The back door is the main entrance as can be seen by the steps, worn into a hollow by many years of nailed boots. Below the house the byre stretches into the field and, below that, the pig sheds and midden.

It is what they call a mixed farm with milk cows, some pigs, a small flock of sheep and a scattering of hens which scratch round the yard at one's feet. I imagine that it is not an easy life, rising in the dark and finishing long after dusk once they have finished the evening milking and bedding the cows for the night. I think they will make most of their own fodder apart from some concentrates to boost the milking. As well as the baled hay they have several stacks of oats which are probably thrashed when the travelling mill comes round. There is a field of kale down by the river and an acre of turnips.

My main concern for Mick is the lack of intercourse with youngsters of his own age. The farm is somewhat isolated and many of the others are held by elderly people. Still, I believe that this family attend church regularly and it may be that he will encounter other Christian youngsters there. To the best of my knowledge there are no other children fostered in the valley unless they are Catholics from Smyllum Orphanage in Lanark. Mick does not make friends easily and tends to keep himself apart from his peers, regarding them with suspicion and distrust.

The family consists of an elderly couple, of which the husband is almost crippled and unable to help on the farm, and a son who is fit and strong. The mother and son share most of the work. There is a daughter, Rose, who has recently returned from the mainland and who helps with the chores. However, she strikes me as being rather feeble-minded and painfully shy. The family attend the local Free Church and are committed Christians, a characteristic which should please the Committee.

I am confident that Mick will thrive here – certainly it is better and safer than working as a bookie's runner! His mother, in any case, is in hospital with TB and her recovery from that dreadful disease is far from certain.

I hope to leave for the mainland tomorrow and will call on you later in the week.

Yours sincerely,

George.

Chapter 18

Rose stands outside the village shop, fingers twisting the baler twine which acts as a belt round her grubby raincoat. She looks down at her welly boots caked with cow shit from the byre.

That'll not do, she mutters.

She walks across the road, plucks some grass from the hedgerow and wipes off the worst of the muck.

That's better. Nellie won't see the feet anyway. Half blind old cow.

She wipes her boots on the bank and turns back to face the shop and marches toward the door.

The doorbell tinkles as she steps into the gloom. Old Nellie squints at her through her thick spectacles.

'Morning Rose. What brings you down so early? Milk away?'

Not early. Milk away same time as always. Saw Duncan heaving the milk cans on to the transport box behind the tractor. Clanged against each other as they bounced up the road. Round tops like flat hats.

'Have you got crepe bandages?' she asks.

'Oh I don't know. I'll need to look. Have you hurt yourself?'

Nosey cow. Say nothing. None of her business. Look at the varicose veins in her legs as she steps up on the chair to search the top shelf. Like ivy stuck on a tree, sucking the life out of it. No wonder she's so pale. Fingers clawing the shelves, shaking like pigs' ears.

'Here we are. I'd forgotten we had any. How many do you need? Is it an ankle that's bad?'

'How many in the box?'

'Let's see. Eight I think. Yes, eight.'

'I want the box. How much is that?'

'That's an awful lot, Rose. Are you sure? All those.'

Say nothing. None of her business. Squinting at me through those thick glasses like the bottoms of bottles. Hair sprouting from her nose too.

'How much?'

'I don't know. I'll have to look it up. You can pay again.'

'No. Pay now. How much?'

Mustn't be nervous. Pay now. Don't be rude. She might tell.

'Wait a minute then.'

She's cross. Her mouth is all tight like a cow's hole. She bends down and lifts a big book and bangs it on to the counter. Daddy does that with the Bible after breakfast before prayers. Our Bible is bigger and heavy. His breath goes puff as he bangs it down on the table and his hands shake. Her fingernail shakes too as it slides down the page and stops at a number.

'Aye. Here it is. That'll be two shillings.'

Feel in my pocket and hand her my ten shilling note. She stares at it lying on the counter.

'Looks like it's been in the mincer. Did you make it yourself?'

How make it myself? Stupid cow. Made by the bank on the mainland and been kept safe in my secret tin until I put it in my pocket. She flattens it out as if she was going to iron it and presses a button on the till and it goes ping and the drawer flies open and she puts my money in under a clip. Her fingers scrabble among the coins and she hands me my change and I go to walk out.

'Don't forget your bandages.'

Feel my ears going red. Mammy yells at me when I forget things. I turn back and lift the box from the counter. Nellie is shaking her head.

Outside it is cool and quiet.

Rose removes the bandages from the box, flings it over the thorn hedge and stuffs the bandages one by one into the front of her coat.

No bloods for two months now.

She tilts her bicycle away from the wall and tries to push it forward but the back wheel skids along the gravel. The brake pads have stuck to the rusted rim. She squeezes the lever three times but they don't release. Lifting the back of the bike by the saddle she thumps it hard on the road. Her lips are curved in panic with pale patches below her cheeks.

Stupid bike. Never works right now. Shining new it was then on my birthday. Gleaming handlebars, black tyres that smelt like tar, lamp clamped on to the bird bracket, pump with the floppy nozzle.

Where's the pump now? Daddy smiling with pleasure. His present not hers. So strong then he could heave hay bales on to the trailer with one hand and fork sheaves to the top of the mill with one flick. He could do anything.

'Not now,' she says out loud, the sound of her own voice a shock in the silence. A wren flitters in the hedge.

Shush. Mustn't speak. They laughed in the school at that. Going to be late and they'll shout me useless they'll say. Bloody bike! Don't swear. Go to hell if you swear and burn forever in the flames. Wash your mouth out with soap again if you swear, girl. Bloody bike!

Kicks the wheel and the brakes open their jaws.

Big brother Duncan watches me ride into the yard. Wee piggy eyes under black brows and big red face like bladder and chin not shaved. Standing with basket of turnips. Why standing? Usually running everywhere like a dog chasing tail.

'Where were you?' he says.

'The shop.'

He knows I go to the shop sometimes..

'Why didn't you say? You're supposed to say.'

'Forgot.'

'Stupid girl. Bloody brainless. You were told to muck the calves. Go and get on with it.'

He turns away and hurries into the byre.

He swears and he gets away with it. Why can he swear and I can't? Swear in my head. Bloody, bloody, bloody. But not the F word or the C one. Never those.

She swings her bike into the tractor shed and parks it beside the trailer but doesn't go to muck the calves. She sneaks into the house by the front door, tiptoes up the stairs to her room, slips the bandages from her coat and hides them under her knickers in the drawer. The drawer squeaks and she stands rigid, listening. Holds her breath, waiting for Mammy's voice.

Silence. Breathes again. Back down the stairs, listening all the time, and out into the yard.

'Nobody heard,' she says aloud as she hurries round to the midden to get the barrow.

The sides of the barrow are caked with dung but the shafts are clean. She plucks the graip from the midden, drops it in the barrow and wheels round to the byre. Cows are all chomping turnips. The nearest raises its head to look at her, its neck chain clinking on the stall side. She stops and stares back at it.

'Bessie. Big sad eyes Bessie. Beautiful girl Bessie. Aren't you?'

'Get on with your work!'

She steps back startled. Duncan shouting further up the byre. Piggy eyes above a cow's back. Frightening. Mammy hit her once, slapped across the face, knocking her into the grip with the cow shit. Lying in the shit looking up at an udder, her ear singing and cheek burning. She hurries over to the calves' pen. They know her and crowd against the rails.

Her job to feed them at the end of milking. Teach them how to drink from the pail, her finger in the milk pretending to be a teat. Get them to suck her finger. That's the best bit, their rough tongues round her finger, sucking

Herds the calves to the back of the pen with a wooden flake and starts to fork the straw bedding into the barrow. Heavy layers of dung stinking with splashes of pale scour.

They'll not find them. Bandages are safe. Mammy doesn't look in the drawers. Asks if I've washed my towels every month that's all. Have to get up early and wash them before the men come down. Caught once.

'You cut your finger?' Duncan asked.

Did not say. Saw his face glow when he knew.

Mammy told me what it was. Like a heifer for the bull she said. A beast can't get in calf without the bull. Saw the bull mount a cow its pizzle like a worm with a sharp nose going into her. Grunting and snorting through the ring in its nose and white froth on its lips. A bit like the man groaning.

Don't think about that.

She fills the barrow and wheels it out to the midden. The midden planks are slippy and steep with deep dung on either side. A bit too far one way, a slight mistake, and the wheel sinks into the mire and the whole load sticks. She takes three steps back and charges at the first plank. The rubber wheel bumps over the edge. It takes all her strength to keep the barrow going up the slope, her boots slipping on the wood worn smooth by constant use. One, two, three planks and the fourth is level. She reaches it and tips the barrow, her breath smoking in the cold air.

See! I made it. Bloody Duncan. Piggy eyes. Look, there are the wild geese. Listen to them honking. A 'V' in the sky, wings flapping, necks stretching like ladies. Where to?

Not to the river. No, too high for that. Not to the peat bog. Maybe the home farm, the big rape field. That'll be it. Waddling through the rape on web feet like fat Nellie in the shop. Nosey cow. Trying to find out.

'Rose!'

She jumps back, one boot in the dung.

'What are you doing? Standing there like a loonie. Get on with your work'

Where did he come from? Duncan spying on me. Must have left the byre just to look. Hate him. Long drink of pish. Mustn't swear. Soap. She did that. I remember the taste. She bent me over the sink and scraped her nails on the yellow soap and rubbed it on my tongue and I was sick in the sink.

'What are you doing, woman?' Daddy said and she said nothing and looked at him hard and walked away.

He got a towel and tried to clean my mouth but soap was there for days.

She wheels the barrow back down the planks and goes back to the byre.

'Never mind the calf pen,' Duncan says, 'I'll finish it myself. Go and cut kale.'

'The boy's job. He can do it.'

'The boy'll be bruising oats. Just do what you're told.'

'Where's the knife?'

'Where it always is, you loonie. You know fine where it is.'

'No.'

'In the bloody trailer.'

Piggy eyes, face like skelped arse. Handle of the hedge knife wet and cold. Blade shining black and sharp as razor. Not too heavy in the hand. Swipe the head off dead cow parsley. Swish. Smell the pig shed from here on the way down to the kale field. Smell in the nose sharp, smell in the clothes never leaves, smell in the hair, like a cloak wrapped round you. Ice in the tractor tracks going down to the kale. Hit it with the hedge knife and it splinters in a star. The field by the river with thorn trees and fence wires hung with sheaves from the harvest when the brown flood water washed the stooks away. Brown water swirling and floating with branches and leaves and a lamb drowned and its wee feet trying to run. Bad flood. Daddy by the pig shed looking down watching us dragging sheaves from the water, cold water round my waist, hauling at my coat, and my fingers freezing. So sore.

Big leaves of kale flop down with frost. Stalks craggy and thin like Daddy's legs. Swipe them with knife and the leaves shake wet all over my legs. Swipe them and cut through and hold them and cut off the leaves and lay them in rows. Legs wet and freezing.

Boy's job. Bloody boy. In warm by the bruiser.

After tea tonight. That's when. Upstairs. Say nothing.

Chapter 19
MICK

She's strange. Don't mean she's daft or anythin. Just strange. The lift doesn't go to the top floor if you see what I mean. Most times she's normal. You wouldn't know there was anythin different but whiles you see her stop sudden an stare into the distance like she was seein a ghost. Like yesterday she was hangin out washing and she flapped out a pair of long drawers, makin to peg them up, but just stood there with her arms stretched out like a scarecrow starin over the valley. Fairly jumped, though, when that mother of hers yelled at her. Dropped the drawers in the mud.

Always wears the same raincoat, wet or dry, sunshine or rain, an old blue burberry thing like you wear at school with the cuffs all frayed an no buttons. Ever since she came back to the island she wears it. Don't know where she was. Somewhere on the mainland workin. Can't think what kind of job or why she came back. If it was me I would stay over there. Imagine coming back here. No picture house, no football, no dance halls, no shops, no trams. Jesus.

Don't know why she's so pale. You'd think that workin outdoors she would have a red face like the other girls here but no. Big dark eyes like a Jersey cow, always watchin, flickin about. Sometimes they look at you, starin, an other times she ducks her head an hides under the hairy brows. I've never seen her hair. Always hidden under a headscarf tied tight under her chin but it'll be black like her brows an that fluff over her lip. I like her smile. Doesn't happen often but, when it does, it's like a different face, like she pulls a mask on an her eyes come alive an her cheeks have dimples. I don't fancy her. Don't get me wrong. Not my type at all.

Oh shit. Here he comes. Big numpty. Bouncin down the yard on his tractor. The only time he smiles is when he's sitting up there with his hands on the wheel. Swings her round an backs her in by where the bruiser is. He'll wait for me to lift the drivin belt an slide it over the pulley at the back of the tractor an he'll move the tractor forward to tighten the belt, switch on the power an there'll be a wild clatter so that I can't hear a word he says as the belt flies round. He'll jump off his precious International an shout at me to get on with it.

I don't mind bruisin oats even though the dust makes me choke an I'm deaf as a post after. It's dry in the shed an away from the wind. I like the feel of the grain on the big shovel when I fill it from the sack an toss the oats into the bruiser an I like the smell of the crushed grain. It's like porridge cookin. When the sack below the bruiser is full I swing it into the corner. One and a quarter hundredweight sacks an I can swing them around like chaff cos I'm as strong as an ox, arms like a gorilla, back like a bull. That's why he keeps me here. Has threatened to send me back to the home a couple of times. If he does, it'll be because of her.

It was his idea to put her on top of the mill with me.

The travelling mill came to the stackyard every winter. Half the height of the stacks an long enough to get stuck in the farm gate, it left hardly any room in the yard for the threshed straw spewin on to the cobbles. To show I was hardy I bagged the job of lousin the sheaves. Liked the excitement of that place on top of the mill, the throbbin of all that machinery under your knees an the way the thresher snatched at the corn in your hands. Dangerous. You could lose fingers if you were careless.

Anyway he put Rose up there beside me. Thought it would be funny, that it would embarrass us so that the men helping could laugh.

The men forkin sheaves from the stacks made dirty jokes about us. I could tell by their stubbly grins an the way they leered at her but I couldn't hear what they said an she never looked at them. He made it a rule, us up there as the mill went round the neighbourin farms, him roarin with laughter

'Loonies to the lousing! Up you go.'

The men would laugh and we would climb the mill, glad to be away from them.

I watched her slicin through the twine, her fingers, thick with milkin, grippin the corn like hawk's feet. Whiles I wanted her to

104

look up at me but I knew that she would never risk that. She wouldn't want the men to see in case they guessed what had happened.

I remember her kneelin on top of the travellin mill, a cloth tied round her nose an mouth, cuttin the twine bindin the sheaves an feedin them down into the thresher. She was good at it. The two of us above the whirrin blades, cut off from the others by the clatterin belts an the height of the mill, up there in a cloud of corn dust, her eyes streamin an her cheeks smudged black. In that baggy coat she was just like a man.

I knew she wasn't.

She came to the bothy one time. It's not really a bothy. An old farm cottage with an upstairs but I don't go up there. Live in the kitchen where it's warm an have a bed in the corner. They said they would feed me in the farmhouse but I didn't want to eat there. I did the first week. Jesus. The old boy took down the bible an read a bit before we ate an then they said grace an nobody spoke the whole meal time. Jesus it was awful. The old boy's hand shakes so much he spills his soup down his shirt. The spoon rattles in the plate. Poor old sod.

He pours his tea into his saucer an slurps it an the old dear she glares at him through her thick specs. After I came he was the only one who spoke to me kindly but not at meal times.

That's why I said I would do for myself.

There's a calor gas cooker an a fire that heats the water. They said if I was going to do for myself, I would have to buy the gas cylinders so I don't use much if I can help it. There's a bathroom an sometimes on a Sunday night after I light the fire early I have a bath.

It was a Sunday when she came in. Just opened the door an walked in, no knockin or anythin. I had just sat down an lit a fag.

'You shouldn't smoke,' she said.

'Smoke if I like. My house.'

'It's not your house. We just let you use it.'

I took a deep drag an blew the smoke at her.

'You going to go and tell, eh? "That awful Mick smokes in our house, Duncan." You going to say that?'

'Mammy'd kill you if she knew.'

'I'm not afraid of her.'

She stared at me for a while an then walked over to the bed an sat down.

'Do you not have sheets?'

'What do you need sheets for? I sleep in the blankets.'

'Filthy beast. Everybody has sheets. Maybe you wet the bed.'

'Christ's sake! Of course I don't wet the bed. Do you?'

She didn't answer. Just stared at the pillow an stroked it with one hand an put the toe of one wellie behind the heel of the other an started to push it off.

'Do you want to have sex?' she said.

I swung round to look at her face. She was smilin as if she meant it. I stubbed out the fag in the shoe polish tin I used as an ashtray. Some boys would have helped her undress an shagged her without thinkin but I was frightened of her like you'd be scared of a witch. You couldn't tell what she might do. Maybe she was only trying to catch me out an would get me on the bed an then slap my face an run out laughin an make me look a numptie. Maybe she'd strip off an we would be shaggin an Duncan would walk in. Christ he'd go daft an hammer hell out of me an call the cops an I'd be clapped in a cell before you could wink an sent back to a home. I did think about it, though, just for a second. What it would be like kissing her with that furry lip an what she would be like stripped under that raincoat but then I thought of Mary. I stood up and opened the door.

'You shouldn't be here. You'd better go home.'

She stamped her foot to put on her wellie and walked past me. She was still smilin in the same way.

'I'm going to tell them,' she said, 'Tell them you had sex with me.'

***

'Have you not finished yet?' he roars over the clatter of the belt an the noise of the engine.

'Aye'

He switches off the power, jumps on to the tractor an reverses till the belt's slack. I slip it off the pulley an start to roll it up. I was thinkin he would drive away but he pulls forward and stops the tractor. He comes back into the shed an he's frowning an his eyes are that hard way when he's cross. I don't like that.

'You took your time, boy. I could have bruised two ton in that time.'

'I was as fast as I could.'

'Not fast enough. Lazing about again, eh? Just can't leave you for a minute. Anyway you'd better buck up, son. Inspector's coming tomorrow. You don't want to go back to the home, do you? Do you?'

'No.'

'Well then. You can go up to the top field and sned some swedes till lunch time. I know where you finished last time so don't think you can sit on your arse.'

He turns an hurries away as if he's late for a bus.

I fetch the knife an head up to the turnips. It's great up there. You can see right over the sea to Ireland. Aye an you're on your own cos he doesn't come up there much, only when he wants the trailer filled with neeps. You go up across the road and through the jaggy whins.

Sometimes the ground's so hard with frost you have to kick the neeps out of the drills but you get into the swing of it. Lift the neep, four whacks of the knife to clean the bottom, one whack to cut off the shaw, one toss on to the row. Sore on the back, though, howkin them out of the ground. Still, look behind you and there's a row of snedded neeps as neat as you like.

Cold on the hands today. See, there's Ireland over there and Cameron's boat out for his creels. Like one of they wee skeeter things you get on a pond. Better not stand here, though. On with the job.

Inspector tomorrow. Much good that'll do. Didn't do any good at the Munro's. You can't say anything. They just clype to the folk and you get it the next day.

Christ, the Munros! Her buryin my face in her udders and pretendin to cry.

'Poor wee lamb.'

Smell of sweat and sour milk and fag smoke.

POOR WEE LAMB!

Slash her head with the knife! Slice it open! Whack! Purple skin and yellow flesh.

That's good. Whack another. Hold it up by the shaw and slice it. His head this time.

Whack! Brilliant. Straight through. Another. Duncan this time. Bang! One day I'll do it. Open his head out. Just like that. I will. The bastard.

Chapter 20

Door crashes open an he comes stormin in an over to the bed an grabs me by the hair. I can hardly see him in the dark.

'Get outa your bloody bed!'

He hauls me out o the bed an pulls me outside an across the yard, me in nothin but my Y fronts. The muck squeezes up between ma toes an ma feet are freezin. The light is on in the pig shed an he pulls me in an shoves ma head over the side o the pen.

'Look at that you wee bastard!'

Jesus Christ! Five o the big pigs lyin stretched out dead.

He bangs my head against the pen.

'What did you do to the meal, eh? What did you put in it?'

'Nuthin. I never did nuthin.'

'You're a fucken liar.'

Christ he must be mad. I never heard him swear like that before.

'Leave me alone. I never did nuthin.'

I locks ma fists round his hand holdin ma hair an digs in ma nails an he lets go an I runs back to the house an bangs the door shut an slides the bed against it. I'm pechin like a racehorse an ma heart's thumpin in ma head an ma hands are shakin. I'm listenin for him to come. I grabs the poker from the old fire an waits for him. I'll break his fucken skull if he gets in.

He doesn't come though. I turns on the light an gets ma clothes on an lights a fag. Ma fingers are still shakin.

I'll have to run, get outa here. But where'll I go. It's a bloody island. I goes to the old chimney an gets down ma secret tin. A couple o quid from Frankie. Kept it from they bastards in the home. Clever boy, Mick. Enough for the boat. But shit! The polis'll be watchin. Where'll I go? Supposed to be a cave on the shore. The byreman up the road said there was. Go there.

Why's he not comin?

I fills the kettle an lights the gas. Make a mug o tea an a piece an jam. Wonder where's the cave? Up to the turnips an out on to the hill where the bullin heifers are an head for the shore.

Engine starts for the milkin machine an I can hear them rattlin about in the byre.

Funny they're not shoutin for me. Maybe they've sent for the polis. Blame me for killin their pigs.

It's daylight now an still they've not come. Finished my tea an rinse out the mug.

I hear a car or somethin comin into the yard an a stranger talkin to Duncan an they go into the pig shed. Now would be the time to scarper. Get ma oilskin jacket, fags, matches, money an go.

I opens the door an there's the old boy hobblin across the yard on his two sticks.

'Mick, my boy, can I come in? I can't stand long on these legs of mine.'

I goes back in an he comes too. He near falls on the step an I grabs his arm an steers him in.

'Can I sit on the bed?' he says.

'Aye. Sure.'

He hobbles over an sort o falls on to the bed.

'Tell me, Mick, what happened with the pig's meal?'

'Nuthin. I bruised it an bagged it an fed it to the pigs.'

'You did nothing different, nothing out of the ordinary?'

'No.'

'No chance dirt got in or any foreign bodies like a dead mouse?'

'No, I would have seen it.'

'I believe you, Mick. I'm sure you wouldn't do a beast any harm deliberately.'

'I wouldn't.'

Duncan comes to the door an frowns at his old boy.

'Come out here, Mick.'

I looks at the old boy an he nods me to go.

I goes out an there's this big thin man in green wellies an a barbour coat.

'Come and show the vet what you did with the meal.'

I goes to the bruisin shed an they come too. I points to the bags of barley.

'I bruised it an bagged it and fed it to the pigs.'

The big man goes over to the bags an takes a handful of barley.

'There's your trouble, Duncan. The barley's got mould. Look. You can't feed dodgy barley to pigs. Sensitive animals pigs, bad barley, aflatoxins, enteritis. Simple.'

Duncan's near greetin. Tips back his cap.

'You should have noticed, Mick.'

'No,' I says, 'you should have noticed. You opened the bags.'

I am that mad I could spit in his face. I don't care what I say. He's not goin to blame me for his pigs.

'It's not the boy's fault,' says the old boy. 'You should have checked yourself.'

Jesus. Somebody on my side.

'Send me your bill,' says Duncan to the big man an walks away. The old boy hobbles after him an the big man goes to his car. I gets the barrow an start muckin out the byre.

'Here,' he says an gives me a pick an shovel, 'in the stubble down the by the river. Start digging. A hole big enough for the pigs.'

'For the pigs?'

'Yes and don't be all day.'

'That's a big hole.'

'Your fault. You bury them'

'Not ma fault. Your dad said so.'

He goes to take a smack at me but I picks up the shovel in ma two hands like I was goin to hit him an he backs off.

'Get on with it,' he says an walks away.

I goes down to the stubble and leans on the shovel. Glad I stood up to him. Ma woulda been proud o me. I throws off ma jacket an spits like a man on ma hands. Look at they muscles in the arm, Mick. Not bad, eh? Twirl the hands round an see them squirm like snakes. Must be quite strong. Maybe that's why he backed off. Big yella bastard.

Wish Mary was here. Could show her the muscles. Show her how I can swing the sledgehammer when I'm splittin big logs. Eight foot logs lyin flat an I split them with a steel wedge. What a clang when the hammer hits the wedge. Like a riveter in the yards. The log sorta groans when it splits. Good stuff. Wish she was here. In her red shoes. That'd be a laugh. Red shoes all covered in shite. One day I'll go back. Go back an find her. I will.

I starts diggin the hole. Top sods's okay an then bloody gravel. Have to use the pick.

Spit on ma hands an grab the handle. Swing it an it bounces in the gravel. Christ this is goin to take ages. His fault the pigs. He should be doin the diggin. If he was here, I'd fell him with the shovel. The lyin bastard.

Oh God! Here comes Rose. What does she want? She's hurryin too.

'There's a man to see you. Duncan says you're to come now.'

'What man?'

'A man. What are you doing?'

'Diggin a hole. What's it look like?'

'Why?'

'To bury your brother.'

'He's not dead.'

'I wish he was.'

'I'll tell him.'

'I don't give a shit. Tell him.'

'Don't swear. It's bad. Why are you digging?'

'To bury the pigs.'

'What pigs?'

'The pigs that died. Your brother fed them rotten meal and killed them'

Jesus she doesn't know. They haven't told her.

'No. Duncan wouldn't do that. He loves the pigs.'

'Well he did and they're dead.'

She starts to greet and runs away. Maybe I shouldn't have said. Better go up but they'll say I've hurt her. It's sure to be ma fault she's greetin. Wonder who the man is. Maybe he's come to take me back to the home. Maybe I'll not go up. Maybe I'll wade the river and run. No, Mick. Go and face them like you faced up to him.

I goes up and it's Mr Buchanan in the yard all by himself.

'Hello, Mick. How are you?'

'Fine, sir.'

'Can we go into your house? I'd like to hear how you are enjoying the work here.'

We goes into the kitchen. He looks all round the place.

'I believe you cook for yourself?'

'Yes, sir.'

'What will you be having for tea?'

'I got sausages off the grocery van an they give me eggs an a slice o' bread fried in the drippin.'

'Sounds quite appetising, Mick. I'm tempted to stay. May I sit on the bed?'

'Aye.'

'And what about breakfast? You'll need a good hearty breakfast.'

'Cornflakes an milk an two boiled eggs an toast an tea.'

'Not bad. Do you like the work here?'

'Yes, sir.'

'All of it? There must be some tasks you dislike surely.'

'I don't like diggin holes for dead pigs.'

He looks pleased that I said that.

'Yes. I heard about the pigs, Mick. Mr Irvine told me. It seems you fed them the contaminated meal.'

'That's a lie. Duncan opened the bags. He should have seen that the barley was rotten.

His Dad said that. I just bruised the barley an fed it to them like I was told. It was his fault.'

'Yes. I'm inclined to agree with his father. He seems to be an honest old man. Is the rest of the work all right?'

'Aye. It's good. Better than the Munros anyway.'

'I'm truly sorry about that.'

He told me he was sorry before at the home. He was near greetin that time.

'How do you get on with Rose?'

'Fine.'

'Is she friendly to you?'

'No. She doesn't bother me.'

'I see. And Duncan's mother?'

'I don't like her.'

'Oh and why is that?'

'I don't like the way she shouts at Rose, pushes her about an slaps her sometimes.'

'I'm sure she will have her reasons. It's really none of our business. Do you go into the village at all? To meet other youngsters.'

'No.'

'Why is that?'

'No time. Milkin mornin an night every day.'

'No time on Sunday?'

'Do ma washin on a Sunday and redd up ma room.'

'Do you not go to church with the family?'

'No. They don't make me go.'

'Won't be long till you are old enough to leave. What will you do then?'

'Find my Ma.'

'Yes of course. I think I should tell you that she is in hospital.'

'In hospital? Where? What's wrong?'

'She has trouble with her chest but don't worry, she is making good progress.'

'Where? I'll have to go. Go and see her.'

'You can't do that, I'm afraid. No-one can see her.'

'She must be bad then. I've got to go.'

'It's just not possible, Mick, but I tell you what. I will let you know the moment she is discharged and tell you where she has gone to live. I promise.'

Aye. A promise. They all promise and never keep them. They don't want me to find her but by Christ I will. I'll find her. Get outa this place and go to every hospital in Glasgow.

'I'll find her myself.'

'I'm sure you will. You're an able young man. Well, I'll be off. I will call again to make sure you are all right.'

He gets up an pats me on the shoulder.

'You're a good lad, Mick.'

He's a kind man but he's still one o them. You can't trust any o them. He'll probly tell the old dear what I said about hittin Rose. Och well. I don't give a shit. Gonna stand up for myself now, fight ma own battles. One day they'll let me leave here an I'll go an find ma Ma an get a job with Frankie. Save up an have ma own shop an runners an punters an get a single end with Mary.

Chapter 21

Rose wakens in the dark in the early morning and listens for movement in the house. Satisfied that the others are asleep, she swings her legs out of bed and reaches for the bicycle lamp in the drawer. She does not want to switch on the light in case it disturbs her mother. She turns the knob on top of the lamp and a dim circle of light appears on the wall. She directs it to the tallboy and searches for the crepe bandages, slips her nightdress over her head and stands naked on the floor. Her shadow follows her movements.

She removes the paper from one of the bandages and winds it as tight as she can bear round her swelling belly and uses a safety pin to secure it. A second bandage is wrapped tightly round her breasts. She tilts the mirror on top of the drawers so that she can see the result.

Can't let them see. Hide it. She'd beat me. See her eyes black under her specs, big and black and angry. See her chin shaking. Beat me with a stick, legs, arms, head. Feel pain cracking, burning like fire. Screams "Bad girl, wicked, whore. Sin. Flames of hell." Never know though. Hide it. Kill it. Bury it like pigs. All boy's fault like pigs. Tell them that.

"I love you" man said. Smelly man, horrible. Hands tearing clothes. Don't think ! Wipe out pictures. Scrub them away. Bad man.

She slides on her nightdress, turns off the torch and goes back to bed.

The first her mother knows of the baby is when she hears it cry.

Chapter 22
MICK

I'm bent over cleanin the grip in the byre when he comes stormin at me an makes a swipe at ma head. I ducks an it misses an I lifts ma shovel an clouts him on the shin.

'Ya bastard!' he yells an hops back. 'Rape ma sister! I'll fucken kill you.'

He comes at me again an I hits him in the face with the shovel. He staggers back an there's blood in his eye.

'I'll get the polis. You wait. It's the prison for you.'

He limps away to the house.

I go back to cleanin the grip and fillin the barrow. Glaikit bitch sayin I raped her.

Have to go. Polis'll be here. Fling down the shovel and over to house. Money tin and run.

***

GEORGE

Mathew is driving sheep across the road on to the hill ground as I drive up. The lambs are white against the dark, thick wool of their mothers. I watch his dogs herding them into line. He waves at me with his stick and signals me to go into the farm yard as he follows the sheep up the hill.

I drive into the yard and Bridget is standing on the step just outside the farmhouse door. She looks so different, her face weathered and healthy, her hair tied back in a bun and a spotless apron round her waist.

'Hello, Mr Buchanan. What a lovely day.'

'It is indeed Bridget. How are you?'

'Very well indeed, thanks.'

'I'm afraid I'm the bearer of bad news.'

'Mick again. What's happened?'

'It's a long story. Can we go inside?'

She nods and leads the way into the kitchen. A collie pup waddles across from the fireside and licks my hand.

'Have a seat,' she says and sits at the table herself. The table top is freshly scrubbed white. She seems quite at home here.

'The family with whom Mick is fostered have made a very serious allegation. They have a daughter and she has just produced a baby which, she claims, is Mick's and that he raped her.'

'That's dreadful! How awful! Mick? I can't believe it. Mick do a thing like that?'

'He denies it of course. Indeed denies any intimacy with her of any kind. He says that she came to his room once offering to have sex with him and he sent her away. Says that she threatened to tell her mother that he raped her. I must say I believe him. The baby was full term and it's clear that it was conceived before she returned to the island.'

'So what'll happen to Mick now?'

'He's in the cells on the island. That's where I saw him. Unfortunately he fled from the scene and, of course, that helped to confirm the allegations. I'm sure the Fiscal will drop any charges against him but he can never return to the farm. That's obvious. I will have to find another placement for him.'

'He can come here. I can look after him now and I'm sure Mathew will find work for him on the farm.'

'That would be wonderful, Bridget. The best news I've had this year. Is there room in the bothy for him?'

'No need for the bothy. There's room in the house. Mathew and I are to be married and he would stay here.'

'Splendid! I'm so pleased. I'll have to clear it with the committee but I'm sure it can be arranged. First, however, I will have to return to the island and speak to Mick. I'm sure he will be delighted. I don't know how long it will take to clear up the legalities and make arrangements but I will let you know.'

'You can phone me here.'

'Of course.'

Mathew arrives and hangs up his coat in the hall.

'Mathew this is Mr Buchanan, Mick's Officer.'

'Ah yes. How do you do?'

My hand disappears inside his and is squeezed firmly.

'Well, thank you. I've just been explaining to Bridget that Mick is in custody at the moment.'

He moves over to Bridget and places his hand on her shoulder.

'I'm sorry to hear that. What's the charge?'

'First can I say, I don't believe the allegations? He is charged with rape but I'm confident the Fiscal will not proceed. The girl on the farm where he was placed has had a child and is accusing Mick of rape. However, when the child was conceived she was not on the island so it is not Mick's offspring. The girl is half-witted and would make a very poor witness so the Fiscal will have to take that into account. I am convinced that Mick is innocent. The result of this affair, nevertheless, is that Mick can't return to the farm.'

'No. I can see that.'

'Could he come here, Mathew?' Bridget takes his hand and looks up at him, ' He's not a bad boy. Please.'

'I know how much he means to you. What do you think Mr Buchanan? Do you think he would settle here?'

I am not used to being asked for advice but, meeting Bridget's pleading eyes, I feel bound to give my opinion.

'He is a good worker and, before all this business erupted, he was doing well on the farm, living independently, cooking for himself and keeping his accommodation clean. He was treated cruelly at the previous placement and ran away to find his mother. He has always shown that determination to find her. In spite of the present circumstances, I feel that he is a good lad who deserves another chance.'

'I see. Much would depend on what he thinks of our relationship. He may not approve, he may take a dislike to me. He may run away. He seems to do that when the going gets tough.'

'He had every reason to escape from the previous farm and it looks as though he had no choice on this occasion. He didn't run away when he lived with you Bridget, did he?'

'No. Never. He was a great help about the house.'

'Well, let's give it a try. Only a trial, mind.'

Her eyes shine with tears and she squeezes his hand. I can see he is very fond of her and she of him and he strikes me as a kind, gentle person – just the kind of man to deal with Mick. Certainly very different from Munro and young Irvine.

'Remember it will depend on the decision of the Fiscal and my own Committee. Some members may be quite shocked by these allegations and, regardless of the Fiscal's view, may insist that he should be in secure accommodation. I will do my best to persuade them against such a course and I will speak to the Fiscal.'

'Can't thank you enough,' says Bridget.

***

There is a red rubber mattress in the cell, a couple of blankets and a pillow and very little else. Barren and bleak.

Mick is standing against the wall, one hand holding up his trousers as they have removed his belt. He is taller and stronger than the boy I left at the Munros and possesses an air of defiance which actually pleases me. For the first time I notice his resemblance to his mother in the long face and striking blue eyes. The constable brings me a chair and bangs the metal door shut.

'Well, Mick. How are they treating you?'

'He's listenin at the door.'

We wait in silence till we hear the footsteps leaving.

'I've spoken to your mother.'

He pushes himself off the wall.

'Is she okay?'

'Better than ever, looking really well. She's living on a farm in the Pentlands.'

'What's she doin there? Thought she was in the chest hospital.'

'She was but she seems to be cured. How would you like to join her there?'

'You're jokin.'

'No. If we can extract you from this mess and if I can persuade my superior that it is wise, I may be able to arrange it.'

He sits on the mattress, smiling and animated.

'That'd be a miracle, mister.'

'I can't promise anything and there is another matter.'

'Oh aye?'

The smile fades.

'She is to be married again.'

'What?'

He is shocked and I can see the inner struggle to process the information. He rises, forgets about his trousers which fall to his knees, catches them and returns to the wall with his back to me. He stares up at the high window above him.

'What's he like?'

'He's a good man, Mick. A sheep farmer with over a thousand blackface ewes and a score of cattle. A gentle, kind man who will look after her. He could use your help on the farm.'

'A toff, eh?'

'I would not describe him as that. He is a hard-working farmer.'

'How did she meet him? Don't get many farmers in the Gorbals.'

'In the chest hospital, He was a patient there too. Believe me, Mick, he's a good man.'

'You said that about Irvine.'

'I was talking about old Mr Irvine and I have not altered my opinion. He is on your side against the whole family. If your case is dropped it will be largely due to him.'

He turns to face me.

'This new man wants to marry ma Ma? Why? What's in it for him? Someone to scrub his floors an do his washin, a skivvy that he doesn't have to pay?'

'I can assure you it's not like that. They are very fond of each other. If we can get you out of here, I will take you to meet him. If you don't like him or don't trust him, we can forget about the whole idea.'

'An send me back to the Munro's or somethin?'

I was prepared for the resentment and hostility but not for the virulence of it and find myself becoming annoyed. Was he really going to toss this opportunity back in my face?

'I'll leave you to think about it. The least you can do is to try it – for your mother's sake. She is longing to have you with her again. Think of her as well as yourself.'

I leave the cell, irritated with myself for permitting my emotions to interfere with my professional relationship.

Chapter 23

A new man, eh? Ma Ma married. A farmer for God's sake. What's she know about farmin? Bet he's a toff, don't care what Buchanan says. One o they men that swank about in their tweeds an crooks that never saw a sheep. I seen them at sales, they kind, goin on about 'my lambs' or 'my calves' an never got their pink hands up the arse of a beast. Maybe he's no like that, though. Maybe he's all right. He'd better be. Lay a finger on my Ma an I'll slice his fucken face open.

Can't think of her wi someone, a man like. If I think about someone's arms round her or kissin her, ma guts turn over an I shake ma head to get the picture out of it. She's my Ma an I don't want anyone near her. We were a team, her an me. I lugged the ashes down the stair for her an she blacked the stove. I carried up tatties an she made the stew. When she came back from scubbin floors I made her a cup o tea an I can see her sittin by the fire wi her fists round the mug, all red an chapped like, an her knees all skinned and calloused an a fag in her fingers. See her blowin smoke rings an me tryin to catch them an her laughin.

Mind her smile and dimples aside her mouth an her white teeth. Always brushed her teeth, even when we'd no toothpaste she'd do them wi soap. That's a thing. I haven't brushed mine in here. Must ask the screw for a toothbrush.

Beautiful, ma Ma. I mind her hair when she took off her scarf and shook it out. Used to let me comb it out. Soft and silky an black as tar, it smelled of the scrubbin soap she used on the floors an the fags she hung in her mouth. Used to get me to rub her neck an shoulders. She'd a mole on her neck an wee hairs sproutin from it an I said it was a spider an she pretended to scream. She'd go to the baths sometimes and come home smellin of soap and all clean. We had a tin bath in the kitchen an me an ma sister bathed in it an she'd wash our hair an try an keep the soap out of our eyes wi a cloth an rub us down wi a towel after. We'd dry ma hair wi a towel over our head, she tuggin one end and me the other, like a tug o war.

Wish she was here wi me now, sittin on this rubber mattress wi our backs against the wall. She'd believe me. She'd know I never raped the girl. She'd put her arm round me an call me Micheal in the Irish way an tell me stories of the fairies an the banshee an Cuchullain an sing me to sleep like she did when I was wee. Last thing I heard at night was her singin. Used to make herself cry sometimes wi those songs. Saw the tears on her cheeks in the gas light. Always safe when she was there, even wi the barneys in the close on a Thursday night an men bawlin an women screamin outside , never worried. Felt like her arms were round me. Safe like a cub in a den. When I was sick she'd blow on my brow an stroke my head wi her fingers through my hair. Safe till those bastards took us away. Came when she was out.

Different story then. Never safe. Never. Cold, always cold. Even in bed. They'd come at you an you'd no idea why. Grab you by the hair and slash you wi a cane. I mind sittin in the car on the way to the home next to this woman an she had a claw thing as a brooch an I wanted to grab it an tear out her eyes with it. Never spoke the whole way. Huge place it was, like a giant's castle, scary. She grabbed ma arm and tugged me in an past a room full of babies in cots, rows an rows o them. She gave me to this priest an says, 'This is Michael, Father. I'll go and log him in.'

Priest took me to the showers an says to strip off my clothes. I says 'No' and he clouted on the ear so hard I fell over.

'You'll learn to do what you're told, young Michael.'

I stripped off an he took away ma clothes an left me standin stark naked by the basins for hours, freezing an shiverin. He comes back carryin a bundle of clothes an tells me to get into the bath. Stone cold it was, took ma breath away, and stinkin of Dettol or somethin.

When I came out he rubbed me down with a towel.

'Fine body you have there, Michael. Remember its God's creation, a temple not to be abused. If you use it for pleasure, if you touch it for excitement, you will burn forever in the fires of hell. You look as though you don't understand me, Michael. If you play with your willy – this thing here – I will thrash the living daylights out of you to cleanse your soul. Do you understand?'

I never understood why I was to be punished when I played with it but when he played with it he smiled.

That night I kept my head under my pillow so that the other boys would not hear me cry. I thought of her comin home an findin us gone an her rushin round the closes shoutin for us.

'I'm here, Ma,' I kept shoutin into ma pillow.

I shouted an shouted but I knew she wouldn't hear. She'd be cryin and her eyes would be all red an the neighbours would be all round an tellin her about the car.

'She'll find out ,' I says to maself, 'an come an get us. That's what she'll do. It'll be all right.'

I went to sleep thinkin of her comin to the door and takin us home. Every night I told maself that but she never came.

Then I thought maybe she didn't want to, maybe we didn't help her enough, maybe she ran off with some man and forgot all about us an I got angry with her for not comin, really angry. In the mornin I was still angry an I got up an the boy in the next bed bumped against me an I belted him in the mouth an he yelled out an started to cry. Made me feel better. But then this nun came stormin down the dorm an punched me in the face. Jesus Christ I never knew a woman could punch like that, like Randy Turpin, with her fist an I fell on the floor an she kicked me in the ribs. I mind this black shoe wi laces an a pointed toe flyin out from under her habit an the rosary beads swingin about.

'Wee bastard!' she yelled an her face all screwed up wi hate. Made me scared that, the hate, like she was goin to kick me to death, like she'd gone mad, like she was a wild beast, snarlin and spittin. Grabbed me by the hair an dragged me to the showers. Freezin cold an she got as wet as me but she didn't care. Couldn't see right wi specs all wet.

Saw her at Mass later, like she was the kindest, gentlest, holiest woman in the place, wi her head bowed an her fists opened out for prayer. Even her face different, like she was bein the Virgin Mary.

Trust no-one. Not any of them. That's what I learnt in that place. Except ma Ma.

But maybe she's changed, maybe she's different now she's got this farmer. Maybe she won't have time for me any more. I was her man then. I looked after her. I went out an picked coal from the road an helped her to the steamie an peeled tatties. I would've done anythin for her.

It was thinkin o her that got me through that place. I carried her in my head like a jewel, like somethin they could never touch. In bed at night after a thrashin it was her who healed the stripes, blowing on my brow an combin her fingers through ma hair.

I tried to get back to her, to run away. Once, only once. I don't want to think about what they did to me but I never did it again.

Now I'm goin to see her I'm frightened. Maybe she won't like me. Maybe she'll believe that shite about the rape. What'll I do if she looks at me like a stranger, like her eyes were lookin at someone different? I want to see her so much and yet...Christ I don't know what to think.

Chapter 24

'I think a little celebration is in order, my dear. A sherry for you and a wee snifter for me.'

George lifts out a crystal sherry glass from the cabinet, pours his wife a Bristol Cream and hands it to her. She lays aside her darning and watches him suspiciously.

'What's this about?'

He returns to the cabinet and pours himself a large Glenfiddich.

'I have just effected a most remarkable reconciliation.'

He sits opposite her beside the fire and sniffs his whisky.

'Well, go on. Don't keep me in suspense.'

'I must admit I was most apprehensive about the whole affair. As you know the Fiscal dropped the case against Mick but, in spite of that, I had a dreadful struggle convincing the committee to keep him out of residential care. You know what they're like. I have great difficulty controlling my temper in their company but I know that, if I let it get the better of me...'

'I know only too well. You start to shout and lose track of the argument.'

'Well, yes. Anyway, they capitulated in the end and it was agreed that Mick should be returned to his mother.'

'She's out of hospital then?'

'Not only that but she seems to be blooming. She's with a farmer in the Pentlands and he wants to marry her and has agreed to take Mick on.'

'Good God! A boy accused of rape. I know you believed him but you never know, do you? You can never be a hundred per cent certain.'

'In this case I'm certain and the girl's father spoke up for Mick. Anyway, I drove Mick out to the farm, worrying the whole time that the meeting would be a disaster – either Mick would dislike Mathew or Mathew would detest him. Mick sat silent beside me picking his nails and smoking incessantly.'

'Shouldn't be smoking at his age.'

'They all smoke. Anyway, when we reached the farm, Mick's mother opened the door and stood on the top step, clearly uncertain, and Mick also stood quite still beside the car. It was as if time had stopped. For a moment I thought that I had the wrong boy, that Mick was not her son. Their faces were expressionless. It was most extraordinary. It was Mick who broke the spell. "Hello Ma," he said and smiled. She rushed to him and folded him in her arms. It was most touching, the affection between them.'

'I hope it works. He has had a terrible time, that boy. God knows what damage has been done and how it has affected him.'

'He has a chance now. When Mathew appeared in the doorway, Mick stared at him over his mother's shoulder. I could see the suspicion in his eyes. I think Bridget could feel the sudden tension in his body and she turned to follow his gaze. She stepped back and introduced them. Mathew is an astute man, not at all one of these insensitive farmers. By no means. As he came down the steps he had a collie pup in his arm. "Hello Mick," he says, "Your Mam said I'd to keep this wee man for you. Your dog if you want him." He won him over. When they went into the kitchen it was as if they had always been a family.'

'Clever man.'

'Clever and cultured too. Likes music. Opera, not just musicals, but opera. He has records of Gigli and Sutherland and is reading Pasternak. Cultured. A kind, gentle person too. I have great hopes.'

'What on earth does he see in the mother? She can't be high-brow like that.'

'No, not all, but there is a natural intelligence, a spark of...not genius exactly but ingenuity.'

'You like her clearly. I take it that she's quite attractive.'

'She is to Mathew.'

'But not to you?'

'Attractive? Yes but not beautiful.'

'Mmm.'

'Anyway I'm delighted by the outcome. Couldn't have been better.'

***

126

'I have a dilemma.'

'Perhaps you could take some Eno's salts.'

'I'm serious.'

'Of course, dear. You're always serious.'

'I have traced Bridget's daughter, Maeve, Mick's sister.'

Violet flicks through the pages of Woman's Own till she finds the horoscopes.

'I didn't know there was one. I don't think you said. With a name like Bridget I should have known there'd be more, if not dozens.'

'The problem is the girl is in Australia.'

'Good heavens. How did that happen?'

'She was in care in a Catholic institution and they sent her to a home there.'

'Without consulting the mother? I thought they had to have consent nowadays.'

'All very secretive. They're supposed to have Scottish Office approval but somehow they sneak round the regulations. Anyway, she's out there and I have had letters from the girl and her foster parents and therein lies the quandary. Listen I'll read you the letters...

> *Dear Mr Buchanan,*
>
> *We were so surprised when we got your letter. We had no idea that Maeve still had family in Scotland. We thought that her parents were dead and that she was alone in the world. Father Flynn told us that anyway when he brought her from the children's home.*
>
> *Maeve is a lovely child and is such a help to me in the house.*
>
> *Since my stroke I can't do a lot of the housework and Maeve can cook now and can do all the washing. My husband has had to take work in the town because of the drought and is not home till late. Some of our cattle died of thirst and the land was baked hard like rock. In the good years ten years ago when wool was like gold we put money by as did Joseph in Egypt and that helped us*

*through the drought. The sheep suffered too and lambs
died for want of milk. It would break a heart of stone to
see the wee creatures sucking on dry udders. Still, we have
weathered the storm when many sank without trace and
soon my good man will return to us full time. I tell you
all this to show you how we could not have managed
without Maeve. She has been sent by God to help us.*

*She is very happy here and we love her dearly. The only
time she gets upset is when we ask her about her time in
the orphanage here. She will not talk about that.
Otherwise she is a happy, carefree girl. We want to thank
you from the bottom of our hearts for sending her to
Australia and eventually to us.*

*Yours faithfully,
William and Georgina Lovat*

And there is a short letter from Maeve.

Dear Mr Buchanan,

*I am very happy here. My new Mum and Dad are very
kind and teach me lots of things. I go to Mass once a
month and light a candle for my real Mum in heaven
and pray for her. I miss her very much and I miss my
brother. I wish he could come to Australia.
Love, Maeve.*

I am tempted to leave things as they are. The girl seems happy
there, although it is very difficult to tell as the parents may be
standing over her as she writes. Yet the lines about her brother
suggest a degree of privacy. What do you think?'

'I think that Maeve is with good people and is very much
appreciated. Putting her in touch with her real mother is only
going to cause disruption. Clearly she thinks she is dead. Leave
her be.'

'Yes, evidently they told her that her mother was dead. They
lied in other words. But I did promise Bridget that I would trace
her daughter.'

'She's not to know.'

'Yes, but I feel most uncomfortable about deceiving her.'

'Mick is settled, Bridget is settled, Maeve is settled. Leave them alone. You're always interfering. Besides, what would your superiors think? You know exactly what would be said.'

'Yes, I know. You're right. I still feel bad about it.'

'Too much of an idealist. Too much involved with your charges. You always have to be liked.'

'Rubbish. I care for the children.'

'Too much at times. That's my point.'

'You're very hard-hearted.'

'No. Sensible. Objective. Rational.'

Chapter 25
MICK

Every morning now at five on the dot Mathew wakens me. I lie in bed and think of the two hard-boiled eggs that he boils in the kettle and puts in my place at the table. I really hate them but haven't the heart to tell him. We don't speak at that time anyway. Ma is still asleep but she'll have the breakfast ready for us when we come back from the hill.

Most mornings when I reach the top of the hill and look along the Pentlands I can see other shepherds at their marches. Makes you feel you're part of something, like one of a team. I like the good mornings up there. You can hear the curlews calling and sometimes the honk of the wild geese. Other days the east wind'll cut through you and the sleet'll make you tilt your ear into your collar. You give a whistle and the ewes start heading down to the parks. The new lambs behind them stagger through the heather. Have to leave the awful new ones where they are with their mother hanging over them and licking them clean of the birth slime.

Yesterday I came across this ewe hobbling about like she was trying to lamb and her tail end was all bloody. So me and Sweep – that's the pup that Mathew gave me and is now a great working dog – herded her into a stell and I caught her to see what was going on. Her back end was stinking but I put my hand in and found a dead lamb, rotten and all brown. I had to pull it out in bits. Not often that happens but it's the worst job in the lambing. This is my fourth lambing and it's only happened maybe half a dozen times.

The ewes are all moving down quite the thing. I hardly need to whistle Sweep at all. He just ambles along behind them. I'll stop half way down near the burn cos I found this duck's nest with eggs in it and they were cold. Left it a couple o days but she never came back so I started feeding the eggs to Sweep, two every day. He fair enjoys that. I would take them home but I've taken a scunner to eggs cos of the hard-boiled ones.

As we come down the hill I think of my breakfast. Every day the same. Ma makes porridge and fries bacon and eggs and black pudding. I just love breakfast. Mathew and I talk about what we found that morning – maybe a hung lamb or a twin lost in the heather. We get on well. At first I didn't like thinking about him and Ma in the same bed but then I saw how happy she was and I got used to it. There were times when I thought I'd never see her again and I don't forget that feeling. Like she was dead. Times I felt there was no-one there for me.

Like I was alone, no-one to tell I was feard or was hurting. Don't ever want to be like that again.

I think of Mary sometimes. Wonder what she's like and if she remembers me. Wonder if she ever wore the red shoes. I keep planning to go and look for her but there's always something to do here – lambs to feed or clipping or dipping or going to the sales in Lanark with Mathew. I meet girls at the sales but I never know what to say. If I start talking about tupps or dogs, they just laugh. I try listenin to Radio Luxembourg on 208 metres on my wireless so I can get the names in the Top Twenty but I always get them wrong or forget. I don't really like that stuff anyway. I like Jimmy Shand. Maybe Mary'll like Elvis and Bill Haley and that. That'd be a pity. If we fell out over music.

After breakfast we go out and feed any orphan lambs and do the twinning on. Mathew showed me how to skin a dead lamb and put the skin on an orphan like a wee jacket. I didn't believe him that a ewe that had lost its lamb would be fooled into taking on the orphan like it was her own. Mind you some o them aren't so stupid and have to be shut in a wee pen till they take the new lamb. You see them kicking an snorting till they get fed up and give in.

I like the evenings after the dogs are fed. We sit in the kitchen and Ma does her knitting or mending and Mathew reads his books or listens to his records on the gramophone. I'm carving a crook head I made from a tupp's horn. Heated it with a blow lamp and twisted it straight in the vice and now I'm carving a thistle on the end. Sore on the fingers shaping it with my knife but I want to make one of my own. Mathew gave me one of his in the meantime. He taught me to read and write.

One time after the tupp sales he handed me the Scottish Farmer and said,

'Read that to your Ma.'

It was about his shearling winning the top prize at Lanark sale but I couldn't read it right. The next night he said, 'One day, Mick, you might have to run this farm. I won't live forever. If you do, you're going to have to fill in and understand all the forms for the business. It's not easy. Now my nephew is a teacher. How would you feel about him coming round of a night to help you to manage the forms and so on?'

I said I'd have to think about it but Ma said, 'That's a great idea, Mick. I'd be so proud of you.'

That was that.

Anyway I can read the Scottish Farmer and the newspaper. Mathew gave me a book 'No Mean City' and said to tell him what I thought of it. I haven't read it yet. I read about the horse racing cos I remember some of the names and I think about Frankie. Bet he's still at it with a big team o runners. He was some mess that time and took a long time to get over it. He was good to me after that and so was Maggie, his bidie-in. I should go and see them one day. Maybe when I go to look for Mary.

Every day Mathew is looking at the tupp lambs to see if any of them will be fit for keeping whole for the sales.

'See,' he'll say, 'look at that. Legs like a stallion and rump like a rhino. That's what you want, boy. Good legs at all four corners and clean colours on the brow. Look at the way he stands proud with a straight back. Aye, we'll keep him.'

So it's not castrated and fair pampered after the summer, taken inside and fed cabbages, and, near the sale, washed and combed and his face and horns oiled till he looks like a right jessie. Still, it'll fetch big money in Lanark, if Mathew's right. He lets me hold them in the ring for the show. The other herds don't speak to me, even the young ones. They stand and talk to Mathew and don't look at me like I wasn't there. Like I'm not one of them, like I'm different. I suppose I am really. Still, if we get a prize in the show, Mathew hands it to me.

'You watch the judges, Mick. See what they're looking for.'

This year I get to pick a tupp lamb and bring it out for sale.

***

I climb the stair in the close in Crown Street where Mary lived. Don't know why I'm so nervous. The close is different. No smell of pee and the walls are painted. The door used to be always open but it's shut and there's a brass knocker on it. I lift it and chap the door. The noise echoes round the close. A woman opens it and squints out. I've never seen her before.

'Sorry to bother you, missus. I'm looking for Mary.'

'No Mary here, son.'

'She used to live here with her Ma and three other weans. Do you know where they went?'

'No idea. Sorry. The couple we took over from were old folk. What was their name, the family?'

'Doyle.'

'Sounds like a Catholic name. Why don't you ask the priests? One of them might know.'

'Aye. That's right. I'll ask there. Thanks for your help,'

I turn and hurry down the stairs.

That sleekit bastard. What was his name? Father something. Still, I'd better go round and see. With any luck he'll have moved on.

I chap on the door of the priests' house and this young man opens it.

'Hello. I'm trying to find a family called Doyle who used to live in Crown Street. The new lady in their house says that they moved but she doesn't know where. Do you know where they've gone?'

'I'm very new here but Father Begley might know. He's been here for years. I'll fetch him for you.'

It is him. As soon as he appears I recognise him but he doesn't know me.

'The Doyles you're looking for, eh?'

'Yes.'

'And why is that?'

I'm taken by surprise. I didn't think I'd have to say why.

'Friends. Mary Doyle was a friend.'

'Was she now? You didn't go to her school, though. I would

have known.'

'No. I'm not from here. I had a job in the mattress factory and she worked there.'

'So where do you come from?'

'Forth.'

'Forth. You'll know the picture house there then.'

'The Tinto. I don't go to the pictures.'

I pass that test.

'Very wise. Some dreadful films nowadays. Filthy stuff. Are you still in the factory? Surely don't travel from Forth?'

'No, no. I live in Maryhill and work for British Rail.'

'Good steady job. Good pension too.'

'The Doyles? I was asking about the Doyles.'

'Oh yes. The Doyles. It's Mary you're after, isn't it?'

'She was a friend.'

'A close friend was she?'

'Not a girl friend, if that's what you mean.'

'A good-looking girl, Mary. She'll have a husband by now I'd say.'

'She might have. I'd still like to see her. Do you know where she is or don't you?'

'No need to get sharp with me, young man. The Doyles stopped coming to Mass years ago. They left Crown Street and I've no idea where they went. Now I'm a busy man so if there's nothing more, I'll bid you good day.'

'Fine. Thanks for your help.'

He shuts the door and I'm left standing. Don't know where to look now. She could be anywhere. Could be married. Hadn't thought of that. Maybe I shouldn't have bothered but I want to know. I've carried her in my head all this time and I have to see her, see what she's like, see if she remembers me. I mind the time we held hands and went to the shoe shop.

"Mary, The Rose of Tralee," my Da used to sing.

"She was lovely and fair as the rose of the summer,

Yet 'twas not her beauty alone that won me;

Oh no 'twas the truth in her eyes ever dawning

That made me love Mary, the Rose of Tralee."

I hear him singing that in my head. I remember the words.

Maybe I'll sing it to her one day, if I find her. Mary, Mary, where are you?

Could try the mattress factory but I can't spend too long away or Ma'll get worried. We got the clipping finished so there's no rush to get back for the sheep and Mathew'll drive them up the hill at night. Still, I like to fetch in the coal at night and feed the dogs.

I turn back along Ballater Street and go into the factory office. The woman at the desk looks up.

'Can I help you, son?'

'Can you tell me if Mary Doyle still works here?'

'Lots of Marys work here. Don't know about Doyle, though. I'll ask at the pay desk. Wait a moment.'

She goes through to another office.

'Yes,' she says when she comes back, 'Mary Doyle works for us but she's on holiday just now.'

'Oh. Can you tell me where she lives?'

'I'm not sure I'm allowed to tell you that. They'll have her address through there but I think it's confidential.'

'When will she be back?'

'Next Monday.'

'I'll call again then. Can you tell her that Mick Crossan was asking for her?'

'I'll tell the pay clerk.'

'Thanks.'

I walk out into the sun and am happier than I've been since I met my Ma. I feel like jumping in the air. I've found Mary.

Chapter 26

Sleek and elegant, the King George V, a miniature Cunarder with red and black funnels, sails into Oban bay, passing between the island of Kerrera and Dunollie Castle. Her sharp bow cuts through the water and gulls swirl over her wake. As she nudges into the pier, a seaman in the bow tosses a carefully coiled light line to a worker on the dockside. The line, its end weighted with a monkey knot, coils out gracefully towards him and he catches it expertly. The other end is attached to a heavy hawser which he hauls from the ship and hooks over a bollard. A tall man, unshaven and haggard, he coils up the line and flings it back on board. In spite of the heat, he is wearing a heavy greatcoat and a soiled beret. People avoid him as he moves along the pier. He is known by sight to most folk in the town but no-one knows him as a person, a mystery, an enigma. Some say that he is the son of an aristocrat fallen on hard times, others insist that he is a convict escaped from prison and yet others claim that he is a deserter from the army.

SLIGO

It's all right, the cave. I can look out over the sea and watch the boats come and go. I got fish boxes for a bed – Joe Croan's. They stink a bit of herring but they keep me off the earth floor and someone left an old down sleeping bag – Black's of Greenock. I can brew up on a primus stove and even make hash with sausages and packet potato but mostly I get fish suppers in the town. It was a right mess when I found the place with broken bottles and tins and sodden papers and even shit in the corner. Some folk living like beasts.

Seine netters are in just now and I can go down to the pier when they're loading fish on to a lorry and the boys'll fill me a bag with herring. Fresh herring straight from the boat.

I like to watch the baskets of fish swinging up from the hold, all silver and shining in the sun.

I've got work on the pier too, catching the hawsers from the ferries and helping them tie up and leave the pier. Sometimes I'm tempted to take a trip to Mull and see how the Irishman is doing but don't know where he is and anyway I can't risk meeting his folk in case they know O'Sullivan or some of that crowd.

I keep watching for him. The other day I was in the Gents in the station and out of the corner of my eye I spotted this man come staggering in. It was the spit of him and I near wet myself in the hurry to get out cos I'd no gun with me. I went out to the kiosk and pretended to read a paper till the man came out. He was nothing like O'Sullivan but it gave me a fright.

From now on I will carry the revolver in my greatcoat pocket. I went in to the station café and bought a tea and rolled a fag. Why should I worry about the bastard? I could knock him into a cocked hat. A knife would be better than gun. Like the Moroccan soldiers in Spain. Crossed the bridge at night and slit the throats of our guards. No noise. Can't forget that, the dark blood round the sliced gullets. May be I'll get a knife. Could stab him in the street and no-one would see.

Yesterday a load of lambs and ewes came off the ferry at the North pier. The herds and their dogs drove them through the town to the mart and there was one lamb hurt in the crush on deck. It was left all covered in sheep shite but I heaved it over my shoulder and carried it behind the flock Long way to the mart through the square and Gibraltar Street.

'Should have dropped it in the sea,' one of the herds says.

'Still alive. Not much wrong with it.'

'You have it then. Her hip's gone anyway.'

'I've nowhere to keep it.'

'Cut its throat then and put it in the pot. Not much use for anything else.'

Carried her all the way from the mart along the esplanade, past the chapel and the castle gates. Herd said she was a ewe lamb. Call her Dolly after Dolores Ibarruri, "La Pasionara," our heroine in

Spain. "Better to die standing than live kneeling down". Some woman that.

She's in the back of the cave in a pen made of fish boxes. Don't know what to do with her. I plucked some grass but she won't eat that. Could shoot her I suppose. Quick death. I'd sooner she lived, though. Quite like having her here, the wee noises in the night, the eyes looking up at you. Wish she would eat. Maybe I'll ask at the mart what to give her. Should've done that in the first place.

***

Shepherd next door gave me beet pulp nuts and she eats them. Mix them with water in a bucket. He says I can run her along with his sheep in the field but I'll keep her a wee while yet. Good to come home at night and see her there. She bleats now when she sees me.

Bad night last night. Just couldn't sleep. Thinking of the half bottle in the crack in the wall. Bought it yesterday. Don't know why. Well, not true. I know fine. Payday and I'd money and I went in to buy baccy and saw the row of bottles and I felt that hot, peppery taste in my throat and I bought it. Seven years dry now and I thought I was shot of it but its still there, that burning, that thirst for the slug on the back of the throat. Jesus, Sligo, get a grip. Think. Think of the last time, waking up on the cattle deck of the Derry boat covered in cow shit and the beasts standing over you and no idea how you got there. Remember the cold and your feet slipping in the shit as you tried to get up and the terror of not knowing. Think of the nights lying in doorways and guts chewing themselves for food and the demons coming out of the dreams to shake you like jelly. Remember the tremors and the cramps and the puking up the first food in weeks. For Christ's sake, Sligo.

But it's not like that now. You can take a wee drink and that's it. No more. You're a better man now after the seven years, stronger, a man with will power. Look at you. A steady job in the open air. Never late for work. Clear head. You can handle it now. John Barleycorn. Not like the down-and-outs you see in the street, begging for change. Not one of them. You can unscrew the top, swallow and put the bottle back in its place or throw it away even.

Tell you what. Put in the pocket and take it to work so that no-one can steal it. Now that's an idea.

***

How can anyone do that?

I come home and see the smoke coming out of the cave. Can't believe it. They've wrecked the place and killed the lamb. Slit her throat and made a fire with the fish boxes and flung her on top. Sick stink of burning wool and mutton and the smoke's watering my eyes.

I'll kill the fucken bastard who did this. Slice his face open, stab him in the eyes. I'll get him. By Christ I'll get him. The fascist bastard.

It's in the pocket.

Chapter 27
MICK

I went back to the mattress factory and asked for Mary.

'Are you a relative?' the woman in the office frowned at me.

'No. A family friend.'

'She's at work just now.'

'Could I see her? Just for a couple of minutes.'

'We're very busy. A big order to be finished in a week.'

'It won't take long. Promise. It's important.'

'All right. But two minutes, no more.'

She went to fetch her and I stood there like a leek, screwing my cap in my hand like I was wringing a hen's neck.

When she came through I was shocked. I remembered her as an awkward, lank lassie but she had grown and filled out, a beautiful woman. In spite of the overall coat I could see her full figure and shapely legs. Her dark hair was hidden in a headscarf tied at the crown with two wee ears sticking up

'Well, well. Look who it is! Mick the Milkman.'

I wasn't sure if she was pleased to see me.

'Hello Mary. How're you doing?'

'Oh "doing" is it? Not "doin" any more. I'm fine. Just fine.'

'And your Ma? How's she?'

'Trachled as always but doin away.'

'A hardy woman.'

'Aye. She talks about you whiles.'

'I'd like to see her again.'

'Well, call round why don't you?'

'Would she mind?'

'Not her. Takes in any waif and stray...as you know.'

'Still in the same house?'

'No, no. Bigger house in Abbotsford Place.'

'Maybe you could show me. Could I walk you home after work?'

'I might have a fella to walk me home.'

I had thought of that but didn't want to hear it.

'Don't look so sad, Mick,' she laughed. 'Course you can walk me home. I'll need to get back to work or I'll get ma cards.'

'That would be great.'

She hurried towards the door but stopped and turned.

'I still have the shoes.'

Then disappeared.

I walked out into the sunlight and threw my cap in the air.

Scores of women came out of the factory at the end of the day but I spotted her right away. She took my arm as though she was showing off in front of the others. Made me feel like a man, like we were a couple.

'Where've you been all these years, Mr Milkman? I mind they took you away after the raid.'

'On a farm on Arran. They sent me there.'

'Jeez O. Outer space. Far enough away. You're not there now, though?'

'No. On a farm in the Pentlands. I found my Ma and she's married to the farmer so I stay with them.'

'Must be nice out in the country.'

'When the weather's good. Have you ever been?'

'Been to the seaside with the taxies. You know that outing thing.'

'Oh aye. Why don't you come out some day? Come and see the place. Mathew, my new Da, he could come and get you in the Land Rover. Take you out for a day. Away from the town.'

'I can't do that. Take time off work just now. They're way behind as it is.'

'What about a Sunday?'

'Sunday's housework. I clean the house for ma Ma. She's no as good as I said.'

'Oh. Sorry about that.'

We walked on without talking for a bit. I think we were wondering what to say next.

'Have you got a fella?'

'Aye. He's nice. Kind. Clerk in the office.'

'I'm glad.'

'No you're not. I can tell. Actually he's a bit of a Mammy's boy.'

'Would you go out with me?'

'What?'

'I'd like to take you out. Go to the pictures or something.'

'Jesus you're a fast worker, Mick.'

'I've missed you, Mary. There was never a day went by but I thought of you.'

'God you hardly know me. I'm not the wee girl you met back then. Lot o water under the bridge since that time.'

'I want to go out with you.'

She stopped and looked at me. I thought she was going to say no.

'Okay. For old time's sake I'll go the pictures but that's all. Nothin serious. No hanky panky or stuff like that. Just as a friend.'

'Fair enough. That would be great.'

We went to see "West Side Story" in the Gaumont in Sauchiehall Street. She wore the red shoes which fitted perfectly and a tight red jumper and I was really proud to be buying the tickets for two and being shown to our seats in the gallery. Posh plush seats. I'd stopped smoking because of Ma's chest but I bought fags for her and a packet of Maltesers.

When Tony and Maria in the film talked about their wedding I put my arm round her and she didn't mind. I leaned round to kiss her and she turned to let me and she tasted of lipstick and fags but it was magic like an electric shock right through me but warm and soft. Never felt anything like it. Left me feeling like I wanted to look after her, keep her from harm, like she was a wee bird in the nest of my arms.

'I love you, Mary,' I whispered in her ear.

'Silly boy,' she said and kissed me.

Took her to the café after and we sat and held hands across the table.

'Your fingers are all callouses.'

'What do you expect? Fightin wi hair mattresses all day.'

'You don't have to do that. That's no life. Come and stay with me and work on the farm.'

'Don't be daft. I'm no a country girl. Know nothin about cows an pigs and things.'

'I've been thinking.'

'You do too much o that.'

'No. Listen. I can get a job as a shepherd and would get a house with the job and the money's not bad. We could get married.'

'Jesus hold on, wee man. You're one for breakin the speed limit right enough.'

She sat back looking shocked and pulled her hands away. I thought I'd wrecked the whole plan. Stupid, stupid boy. Too much of a hurry. Should have kept it to myself and waited.

'Anyway I couldn't leave ma Ma.'

'She could come with you.'

'Aye right. Recipe for disaster that. Mother-in-law in the house? Naw, naw. Now, sheep-shagger, are you goin to walk me home or what?'

'Course. Here, you keep the fags.'

I'm in the back seat of the bus going home and rolling up the ticket into a tube and really annoyed with myself for talking like that. Fucken eedyit. Course she'd be shocked.

Mind you, she was nice to me on the way back and gave me a long kiss in the close. Maybe it'll be all right in the end. And what'll I say to Ma for God's sake? Can't tell her what I said, saying I'd get a job and a house and get married. Jesus what a numptie.

I do want to marry her, to wake up beside her in the morning with her head on the pillow. Don't know much about women, though. We talked a lot about it in the home but the priests and nuns said sex was dirty and you got leathered if they thought you were playing with yourself under the blankets. We read dirty magazines and boasted about things that we'd never done and tried to imagine what we would do the first time. I wonder what it would be like feeling Mary's skin next to mine. I feel quite horny just thinking about it. Stupid. Might never happen. Wake up, Mick, for God's sake. She might not want to see you again after tonight.

Chapter 28

She's here. Only a weekend right enough but I never thought she would agree. In one way lambing's a good time cos she can help with the young lambs and I thought she'd like that but in another I don't get much time to see her.

I saw her most weekends through the winter and we went to the pictures or round to her house. I like her Ma. No matter how trachled she is, she's always cheery and has time for a blether and asks about the farm and my Ma. She takes in washing so the place is always hung with stuff and smelling of ironing and steam and soap. She tries to embarrass Mary by asking when we're getting married. I wish she wouldn't cos I've never said since that time in the Gaumont.

Some weekends I stayed at home cos she went to the dancing. I can't dance. At least not that kind of dancing like you see on Top of the Pops. Country dancing like the White Heather Club fair enough but all that squirming like a snake stuff's not for me. I hate it those weekends and try not to think about Mary getting all made up and dancing with other fellas. I try to read the Scottish Farmer or watch TV but can't get the picture of what she's doing out of my head. I was always waiting for her to say she'd got another fella and was not going to see me again. It didn't happen though and now she's here. It's great to lie in bed and think that she's just through the wall in the spare room like she belongs here now.

I watch the Situations Vacant bit in the Scottish Farmer and there are plenty of good jobs for shepherds with a house and perks. I don't talk about this though with Mary or Ma. I just think about living our own lives and Mary being my wife. I'm sure her Ma would manage without her and anyway she's thinking of moving out to Drumchapel into one of the new places there. Don't think Mary wants to go though. She likes Abbotsford Place and it's near her work.

There were weeks when I couldn't see her in the winter.

Mathew said it was the worst snow since 1947. The main road was blocked and the snow was over the top of the gates. When we went out in the morning the whole place was silent. You couldn't hear a thing but now and again a ewe bleating. We got most of the sheep off the hill into the fields before it came bad but there was some in a heft at the back that we missed. We went out looking for them and the whole hill in that bit was a blanket of snow. All the burns filled with it. For days we were out searching for the wee holes in the snow made by the breath of buried ewes and digging the beasts out. They'd stagger about trying to find their feet again after being trapped.

I was fair knackered at night with hobbling in the snow and hauling sheep out and didn't think of Mary for a day or two. It was when everything was safe and the road was blocked for weeks that I got more and more restless.

'For God's sake, Mick, cheer up,' Ma said, 'The road'll be open shortly. You'd think the world had come to an end.'

'I said I'd see her a fortnight ago.'

'She'll wait. She'll know quality when she sees it, don't worry.'

Ma was right. She did wait and hadn't gone out with another fella. She'd read about the road being blocked.

I came back from the hill this morning and she was kneeling on the floor feeding a lamb. She was so taken with it that she never looked up.

'It's learned to suck then,' I said.

'I learned it. Your Ma showed me how.'

'I thought it was going to die last night. Foundered with the rain and east wind.'

'Wee spell in the bottom oven does wonders,' Ma said.

She's at the stove cooking breakfast.

'Is Mathew not in yet, Ma?'

'No. He should be in by now. Must have a keb or something. Did you see him on the hill?'

'Just as we left.'

I sat down and watched Mary. She looked really happy with the lamb in her lap. I liked the way her hair fell over her face.

We've had quite a few poorly lambs this year cos some of the ewes are short of milk after the snow. We did feed them but some still suffered.

I have been thinking I would speak to Mary again about getting married. It would be great to run a farm together. She could see to the lambs and the hens and do the cooking and washing like Ma does. Better than that mattress factory anyway. I think she'd like it fine. I look at her sitting there and it feels like we're together already. But you never know. She could turn down the whole idea just like she did before. I just don't know what to do. I know what I want but not how to go about it.

I get up and wash my hands in the sink cos they're stinking of lambing oil.

'Go out and see if there's any signs of Mathew will you, Mick?' Ma says.

She puts my breakfast on the table.

I go out to the gate and look up to the hill but he's not coming yet so I turn back in.

'He'll be lambing a ewe in the bottom stell likely.'

'Aye likely.'

She looks a bit worried.

I eat my breakfast and go out to twin on an orphan lamb. I can see the hill from the twinning pen but still no sign. I get out my knife and skin the dead lamb and slip the skin over the orphan. She's a right skeerie bitch, the new mother, her first lamb, a gimmer, and not a lot of milk. Might be hard to twin so I squeeze some of her milk on to the head of the orphan and put it in the narrow pen behind her. She sniffs it but, as soon as it tries to suck, she lashes out with her foot. The bitch. I feel like giving her a clout on the nose but I talk to her like Mathew does and try again. She kicks again. I lift her tail, pick up the lamb and rub its head in her back end and try again. This time she sniffs it and lets it suck. What a relief!

I thought it was going to be a long battle.

Still no sign of Mathew so I go back to the kitchen.

'I'll take a turn out the hill and see what's up. Likely he's got held up.'

I get the dog and my stick and head out.

I go to the bottom stell but he's not there so I go further up the hill.

I find him in a burn soaking wet and shivering.

'Jesus Mathew! What happened?'

'Thank God you came, Mick. I slipped crossing the burn and I've done something to my hip and can't get up.'

'I'll go and get help'

'No, no. No fuss. Go back and get the tractor and the loose box. Don't say anything. You'll get the tractor as far as the flat ground there. Help me on to the bank before you go.'

He is some weight but I get him out of the water. I can see he's in a lot of pain so I race back and bring the wee Ferguson up the hill. Bit by bit we work our way over to the loose box. He can't stand so he sort of slides across and pushes with his good leg. He howls as I get him into the loose box. I drive back really slowly, trying not to bump him. The dogs follow behind.

Ma is standing on the doorstep and Mary is looking out the window. I stop the tractor beside the steps.

'Jesus Mathew what's wrong?'

'Slipped crossing a burn and buggered my hip. I'll be fine in a wee while. Just need a rest.'

'It's really sore, Ma. He can't stand and he's soaking wet. We'll need to get him in.'

'We can't do that on our own. We'll need help.'

'No. He doesn't want help. We'll do it, you and me.'

Mary comes out and asks if she can do anything.

'Yes, Mary love. Lift his lambing bag and stick and bring them in.'

Ma and I lift him and oxter-cog him into the house.

After the ambulance is gone the three of us are in the kitchen. Ma is sitting at the table turning a table mat over and over. Mary is standing with her back to the sink looking at her finger nails. I'm hanging Mathew's green coat on a peg. Yarmouth, it says on the label. A lamb is rattling its cardboard box by the stove.

'You'll have to manage his hirsel as well as your own,' Ma says after a while. 'Don't think he'll be fit for while.'

'I'll manage.'

'Think I should be gettin back,' Mary says. 'Youse have enough to do without me as well.'

'No. Don't think that, Mary love. You're a great help. Don't hurry yourself. Stay as long as you like. When's your Ma expecting you?'

'Tomorrow night.'

'Well, stay till then at least.'

I don't want her to go at all. We're like a family just now. Mary looks at me as if she wants me to say something, something important, but I don't know what.

'Aye. Go on. Stay, Mary. Ma could do with your help. I'll need to feed the dogs.'

And I leave them in the kitchen.

I go out to the barn and stand there and think Mathew's accident has screwed up all my plans. Can't go for a job now and can't talk to Mary about it either. Shit! All fucked up.

Why did the stupid old bastard have to go and fall? Just when I was going to ask Mary again.

Fuck! I kick the meal kist and one of the dogs cowers away.

'All right, Ben. I wasn't talking to you.'

Maybe Mary could come and live here! Now there's an idea. She could help Ma in the house and help us outside if Mathew's not fit. Wonder if she would. Better than the factory and I'd have her here every night after tea. No need to get married yet. Just be with her. She could come out to the hill and feed the ewes and learn about the farm. We could take walks down to the loch and get gulls' eggs in the spring. She could look after the lambs and roll the wool in the summer and come to the tupp sales with me and I could show her off in front of the other herds and they'd be as jealous as hell. Aye, I'll talk to Ma first.

Chapter 29
SLIGO

Open my eyes and I'm leaning against a slab wall, my cheek hard against it and a guy is walking along it at right angles without falling. Can't be. Christ no. I'm lying on the ground. That's it. Must have been another shell, fascist guns again. My eyes swinging about all over the place. Side's agony. Guts churning. Jesus where is this?

'You okay, pal?'

A voice away to the left somewhere.

I raise my cheek off the ground and try to sit up. Everything swirls about and I feel sick.

'Take it easy, pal. You need a doctor, that's a nasty cut on your head,'

I sit up and touch my head and it's all sticky.

I look up and there's this young fella with a beard and long hair.

'Which Brigade, son?'

'What?'

'You're from Scotland, aren't you?'

'Aye. Course. Where did you think?'

'Where are we?'

'Edinburgh. Sandport Place.'

'Jesus.'

Can't remember. Black hole in the head. Empty. Not Spain anyway. How the fuck did I get here? I sit up with my back against the wall.

'You okay?'

'Aye, son. Thanks.'

'You need to see to that cut.'

'I'll be fine.'

'Okay. Take it easy.'

He walks away and I feel in my pockets for baccy. None and no cash. I need a drink. No you don't, you daft bastard , that's the last thing you need. Need to clear your head. Try to think.

Where's my beret? Gone too. Need a wash. Stand up. Stand up, stand up for Jesus. Lean against the wall. This blond comes along in boots and a miniskirt.

'God, pal, you look like I feel. You okay?'

'You wouldn't have a fag, would you?'

'Aye. Here.'

She sticks a fag in my mouth and lights it for me.

'That's a bad cut. You been on a bender, eh? Better see a doctor and get that cleaned up.'

'Is there a place I can get a wash?'

'There's our great Water of Leith over there. You could wash in that but you'd come out as maukit as you started. Look, come back with me and get yourself sorted. If you stay here the polis'll lift you with that blood on your head.'

'I've no money. Better tell you.'

'Never mind. I can make it up. Never busy this time of day anyway.'

Must be a hooker surely.

'You got a minder?'

'A pimp you mean. No. I work on my own.'

We go round to her place. Some place inside! Like you'd see in the films. Red bed cover, lilac sheets and pillows, huge brass bed, gold curtains. Smells like a rose garden except for the fag smoke. She lights the gas fire.

'Sit down. I'll put on the kettle. Here's a fag and there's an ashtray by the bed.'

She goes into the kitchen and I sit but I can't lie back cos the pain in my ribs. It hurts to breathe even. I light up and try to remember. Christ I mind now and it scares the shit out of me. Glasgow, but not the doss house. Down by the river near Paddy's Bar. Night time. I mind the lights on the black water. I've the gun in my hand. Jesus where's it now? What did I do with it? Didn't fire it, I'm sure. O'Sullivan. That's it. That's him. Jesus Christ I didn't kill him, did I? Tell me I didn't. Surely not. What the fuck happened?

'You look like you've seen a ghost. What's your name by the way? First name'll do.'

'Sligo.'

'That's in Ireland. You're not Irish, though.'

'No. My father was. So I'm told.'

She hands me a mug of tea.

'Drink that and you'll feel better.'

Hope my guts don't puke it back up. They're telling me I've had nothing but liquor for weeks. It's good. Hot and sweet.

'You're not from Edinburgh.'

'No.'

'Didn't think so. Doesn't matter. I'll get a bowl of water to clean that cut.'

She comes back and starts to clean my head. I like the smell of her near my face. Reminds me of Annie Murray in Spain. For a moment the old snake uncoils but that's stupid.

'I've put some Dettol in the water so it'll sting.'

'Go ahead.'

Sting, she said. Have to grit my teeth to stop from yelling.

'You should get that stitched, Sligo. It's a deep gash. Think I can see your skull.'

'It's fine. I hate doctors. They'd ask how it happened and I haven't a clue.'

'That bad. Must have been some party.'

'A party going on for six months maybe.'

'Good God!'

'And I can't remember any of it.'

'That's bad, really bad, if you can't remember.'

'I know. I'll need to stop it.'

'Wicked stuff, the electric soup. Can get a grip of you.'

'Aye. You're right.'

Oban. That's it. In the cave and some bastard burnt my lamb. I remember that. That's when it started. What then? Just a mess like a tub of offal in my head, a slimy mass of guts and glaur.

She goes to empty the basin in the kitchen.

I start to get the shakes. Need to get out o here and get up to go but she comes out from the kitchen.

'I'll need to go, missus.'

'I was going to make you a bacon roll.'

'I couldn't eat anything.'

'No. That'll be right. I've been there too. Here.'

She gets a fiver from her purse.

'I shouldn't give you money, should I, but I can't see you leave here with none. I could say don't spend it on drink but that'd be a waste of time. Up to you but you could do with something to eat.'

'That's good of you, love.'

'Oh aye. Mary Magdalene me.'

'I mean it.'

'Go on. Look after yourself, Sligo.'

I go out and cross the river. A right scum on it right enough. Never even asked her name. Keep walking. Jitters coming on bad. Walk, walk. Jesus I'm weak though. Have to eat.

Enough for some soup and baccy. Aye and a bottle. Don't kid yourself. You were thinking that too. But you can't. Look at the state of you. Brain's mince and lost your beret. You can't, man. No drink. Never again.

And the gun in my hand. What happened for Christ's sake? I must have killed him. I wanted to. Slimy bastard. But did I? Would I not remember the shot? Would I feel it in my hand? Maybe the polis are after me now. Maybe the car'll pull up beside me in the street. Charged with murder. Jesus, man, keep walking. Keep in the crowds. Keep off the main streets. Jesus I need a drink.

Chapter 30

'I'm afraid you'll have to manage on your own for a while, Mick.'

Mathew is sitting in his chair by the stove with a rug over his knees.

'It'll be fine. Don't worry. Neighbours have said they'll help with the gathering and the clipping.'

'Yes. They're good folk. I've been thinking, Mick. I have no children and I'm too old to be having any now. One day this place will be yours. Unless you've any objections that is.'

I don't know what to say. I'm stunned.

'I'm going to speak to my lawyer about it. If I go first, you and your mother will have it between you and, when she goes it will be yours.'

'You shouldn't be talking like that. About you going and that. You'll be out on the hill in no time. You'll be fine. Can we not just carry on as we are, the three of us?'

'That's another thing, Mick. We could do with a bit more help about the place and Mary seems to fit in with us all. Do you think she would give up that dreadful job and come and work for us? I can see you and her are more than friends.'

I could hug him. I've never felt so happy in all my life.

'I'll ask her.'

'It was your mother's idea but I think it's a perfect answer.'

***

I'm on the suspension bridge looking down on the Clyde. I remember coming here years ago with that ex-soldier I met on the railway. He had a kitten that died and he flung it away like it was a dirty cloth. He was good to me, though. Mary's late. Maybe she won't come. Maybe she knows why I want to see her and has chickened out. No, not like her.

Not afraid of anyone or anything. She never says she loves me even when I say that I love her. I think she does, though. I catch her looking at me sometimes and I see it in her eyes.

Here she comes now. Straight from work in her headscarf and overall.

'Why here, Mick? We going throw ourselves off the bridge like? A suicide pact to get our names in the paper?'

'I like it here. You can see the boats.'

'Oh aye. I'd sooner see ma tea on the table.'

'How would you like to pack in the job and come and work on the farm?'

'What? Don't be daft. Me in the country? No dancin, no picture house. Fish out of water. Okay for a weekend but Jesus, every day? Wait a minute, you're serious, aren't you?'

'Mathew wants you to come and work for us. He says one day the farm will be mine. We could run it together, you and me.'

'Jesus, you're not jokin.'

She takes out her fags from her overall pocket and lights up and blows the smoke away into the air. She's frowning at the water as if she could see things there, as if it had the answer.

'You know what, Mick? You're really asking me to marry you, aren't you?'

'No, no. Just to come and work with us.'

'You're a bloody liar.'

'No, really.'

'So you don't want me to marry you?'

I take the fag out of her fingers and chuck it in the river and pull her against me.

'I do, Mary. More than anything in the world.'

Chapter 31

My God it's cold. The east wind that slices through you is gone but there's a fierce frost on the ground. It's still dark but there's a gleam of light over the hills. Leaves on the garden bushes hang down like lambs' ears and there's thick ice on the water trough. My fingers fumble with the bolt on the dog kennel. Mary's still warm in bed and Ma won't be up for another hour unless the weans wake her. Don't like getting up on my own but, with Mathew not able, there's no-one else to do the lambing.

I head out of the yard. My God even the dogs skite on the road it's so slippy, Glad of my tackety boots on the frozen ground. Hard as a rock it is.

Something by the road side. A fox or something hit by a car maybe. Better go and see.

Jesus Christ it's a man! Coat's white with frost and he's not moving. Give him a shake.

'Hey mister. Wake up.'

Feel his face. Cold as ice. What'll I do? Can't go to the hill and leave him.

Give him another shake.

'Hey. Wake up.'

He's still breathing. Hair's stiff with frost.

'Hey, man.'

Eyes flutter open.

'Fuck off,' he growls.

'You can't stay here. You'll freeze to death.'

'Fuck off will you.'

'Come into the house and get warm.'

'Leave us alone.'

'I'm going to the hill. If you're still here when I get back, I'll take you into the house to get warm. Get a cup of tea or something. Okay?'

No reply so I carry on.

What a state to be in, lying out in the freezing cold. Smell of drink too. Don't get many men like that on this road.

By the time I reach the march the sun is up and there's a bit heat in the air. Heather's all glistening with a mantle of frost. I try to whistle but my fingers are so numb it doesn't work properly but the dogs know the routine anyway. Ewes are moving down nicely. I stop and gaze out over the valley. It's beautiful at this time of day. Hardly a sound and barely a movement. A whole world in front of you. There's freedom up here. You feel you could fly, fly out over the valley like the wild geese, over the hills, over the sea, far into the north. Feel the sun on your wings and the wind in your face. Freedom.

I know prison – police cells, children's homes, farms. I am the wee boy tied to the toilet, the runner lifted by the police, the boy arrested for rape. It's all inside me. The terror, the humiliation, the fury. I see all the images but slowly the feelings are fading. Mathew taught me to tame them, to see that, if I didn't, they would eat me away from inside like maggots in meat. And the new feelings, the love for Mary and Ma and Mathew and the children, have grown over the decay of the others. I don't hate the Munros or the Irvines. What they did makes me who I am and I am not angry or afraid or ashamed. Ma is proud of me, Mary loves me, Mathew respects me, the children laugh with me. That says something about the man I have become

The bleat of a lamb brings me back to earth. By the sound of it, it's in trouble. I wade through some long heather and find it in a drain, invisible. A deep drain, it's sides overgrown and the lamb not able to get out. A twin. The mother away with the other, forgetting she'd two. I fish it out and carry it down to her. She doesn't seem grateful. I suppose if you've twins, you might not be delighted to see them both.

I check a ewe in the western stell which had been none too keen on her lamb yesterday and find the lamb sucking away quite the thing. One worry less. I see the ewes and lambs over the road into the fields and then turn to see if the frozen man has recovered. He has moved but he's lying right in the middle of the road and there's a milk tanker hurtling down the hill towards him. With the bend in the road the driver won't see him. I drop my stick and run, grab him by the coat and haul him off the road. The tanker roars past and I'm standing breathless on the verge.

'Christ Jesus. That was close.'

He says nothing but dusts the frost off his coat.

Then I recognise him.

'Sligo! Are you Sligo?'

He glares at me suspiciously. His eyes are red and he squints at me.

'Who are you?'

'You won't remember. We met in a railway hut near Glasgow.'

'Don't remember.'

'Look. Come into the house and get a mug of tea.'

He tries to get up but hasn't the strength. I grab his arm to help but he shakes me off.

He tries again and manages to stand.

'Where's the house?' he says.

'Just over there. Do you need a hand?'

'No.'

He limps along the road and I walk beside him.

***

Sligo stayed with us for a few days, sleeping in the bothy and taking food gradually to build up his strength. His guts rejected the first soup and he threw up in the kitchen. Mary cleaned up and looked after him like a nurse. I loved her for her kindness and tenderness. The children were very wary of him and watched him as if he was a wild animal. He never thanked us for the hospitality but, when he was leaving, he said to Mary,

'What's your mother's name, love?'

'Deirdre. Deirdre of the Sorrows she always said. Why?'

'Just wondered. Doesn't matter. Deirdre. Ay Deirdre. I'll be off then. Tell Mick cheerio.'

'You be okay?'

''Course. Maybe I'll call again one day.'

'Do that. You'll always be welcome.'

That was the day Mr Buchanan came to the door.

'Hello, Mick. It's good to see you. You're looking well.'

He had aged since the wedding and was walking with a stick but he was still wearing the hat that I remember from Munros.

'Come to take me away again, Mr Buchanan.?'

'Never again, Mick. Never again.'

'Come away in. It's good to see you too.'

Ma and Mary were in the kitchen with Mathew.

'Och Mr Buchanan,' Ma said, 'It's so good to see you. How is your wife keeping?'

'Can't get about much with arthritis I'm afraid but she's cheery enough. She was asking after you all. Do call me George by the way. Only the taxman calls me by my surname now.'

'That's kind of her. Please sit down. You'll take a cup of tea?'

'That would be splendid. First, though, I have something to deliver.'

He reached into his inside pocket and produced an airmail letter.

'This is for you, Bridget. It has taken me some years to persuade the Committee but I have kept my promise.'

He handed it to Ma who looked at the postmark.

'I don't know anyone in Australia,' she said.

'Oh yes you do.'

The End

About the Author
Willi Orr

A former shepherd, actor, counsellor, teacher and columnist, Willie Orr was born in Ireland but now lives in Scotland.

Willie has published several non-fiction books, *Deer Forests, Landlords and Crofters, Discovering Argyll, Mull and Iona, 'The Highland Sporting Estate' in Farming and the Land*.

His regular column in *The Scotsman* ran from October 1990 to August 1994 entitled, *The Rural Voltaire*.

He has had several short stories published with Harper Collins, Splinters and Northwords, and has had two plays performed.

Willie was awarded the Scottish Arts Council Writer's Bursary in 1988 and the Scottish Book Trust Mentoring Award in 2010.

In 2019 he published *The Shepherd and the Morning Star*, a remarkable autobiograhpy, and biography of his father.

Also from ThunderPoint
The False Men
Mhairead MacLeod

ISBN: 978-1-910946-27-5 (eBook)
ISBN: 978-1-910946-25-1 (Paperback)

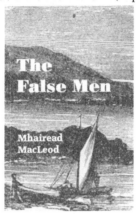

North Uist, Outer Hebrides, 1848

Jess MacKay has led a privileged life as the daughter of a local landowner, sheltered from the harsher aspects of life. Courted by the eligible Patrick Cooper, the Laird's new commissioner, Jess's future is mapped out, until Lachlan Macdonald arrives on North Uist, amid rumours of forced evictions on islands just to the south.

As the uncompromising brutality of the Clearances reaches the islands, and Jess sees her friends ripped from their homes, she must decide where her heart, and her loyalties, truly lie.

Set against the evocative backdrop of the Hebrides and inspired by a true story, *The False Men* is a compelling tale of love in a turbulent past that resonates with the upheavals of the modern world.

'…an engaging tale of powerlessness, love and disillusionment in the context of the type of injustice that, sadly, continues to this day' – Anne Goodwin

The Summer Stance
Lorn Macintyre
ISBN: 978-1-910946-58-9 (Paperback)
ISBN: 978-1-910946-59-6 (Kindle)

Abhainn na Croise, the river of the cross, where the otters swim
and the Scottish Travellers camped for generations, working on
the land, repairing whatever was broken, and welcomed back
each year by the area's settled residents.

Those days are long gone, but Dòmhnall Macdonald, raised in
a Glasgow tower block, yearns for the old ways and the freedom
they represent. When his grandmother falls ill, Dòmhnall
determines to take her back to the Abhainn na Croise one last
time - but times have changed too much.

Instead of the welcome of old, the returning Travellers are met
with suspicion, hostility and violence - and Dòmhnall becomes a
hunted man.

Set in the timeless Scottish landscape, Lorn Macintyre's latest
novel is an intimate portrait of a misunderstood way of life and a
fast disappearing part of Scottish culture.

'The Summer Stance is about racial prejudice; the loss of
the Gaelic oral tradition; and the destruction of the
Scottish landscape, its historic sites and its wildlife through
indiscriminate development.'

The Last Wolf
David Shaw Mackenzie

ISBN: 978-1-910946-39-8 (Kindle)
ISBN: 978-1-910946-38-1 (Paperback)

'So what is the novelist's duty then?'

'Oh, to tell the truth of course.'

But what is the truth when there are at least two sides to every story?

Brothers Maurice and Christopher have not spoken to each other for over 40 years, despite living on the same small island. And nobody talks about Maurice's first wife, Hester – until an apparently unconnected act of vengeance reverberates across the generations and carefully guarded secrets begin to unravel.

Moving from 1930s Capri to Paris, London and the Isle of Glass off the Scottish coast, *The Last Wolf* is a subtly crafted tale of lies and betrayals.

'*The Last Wolf* is an intimate tale of lies and betrayals
lightly and deftly told by a master storyteller.'

QueerBashing
Tim Morrison

ISBN: 978-1-910946-06-0 (Kindle)
ISBN: 978-0-9929768-9-7 (Paperback)

'The first queerbasher McGillivray ever met was in the mirror.'

From the revivalist churches of Orkney in the 1970s, to the gay bars of London and Northern England in the 90s, via the divinity school at Aberdeen, this is the story of McGillivray, a self-centred, promiscuous hypocrite, failed Church of Scotland minister, and his own worst enemy.

Determined to live life on his own terms, McGillivray's grasp on reality slides into psychosis and a sense of his own invulnerability, resulting in a brutal attack ending life as he knows it.

Raw and uncompromising, this is a viciously funny but ultimately moving account of one man's desire to come to terms with himself and live his life as he sees fit.

'...an arresting novel of pain and self discovery' – Alastair Mabbot (The Herald)

Changed Times
Ethyl Smith
ISBN: 978-1-910946-09-1 (eBook)
ISBN: 978-1-910946-08-4 (Paperback)

1679 – The Killing Times: Charles II is on the throne, the Episcopacy has been restored, and southern Scotland is in ferment.

The King is demanding superiority over all things spiritual and temporal and rebellious Ministers are being ousted from their parishes for refusing to bend the knee.

When John Steel steps in to help one such Minister in his home village of Lesmahagow he finds himself caught up in events that reverberate not just through the parish, but throughout the whole of southern Scotland.

From the Battle of Drumclog to the Battle of Bothwell Bridge, John's platoon of farmers and villagers find themselves in the heart of the action over that fateful summer where the people fight the King for their religion, their freedom, and their lives.

Set amid the tumult and intrigue of Scotland's Killing Times, John Steele's story powerfully reflects the changes that took place across 17th century Scotland, and stunningly brings this period of history to life.

'Smith writes with a fine ear for Scots speech, and with a sensitive awareness to the different ways in which history intrudes upon the lives of men and women, soldiers and civilians, adults and children' – James Robertson

The Bogeyman Chronicles
Craig Watson

ISBN: 978-1-910946-11-4 (eBook)
ISBN: 978-1-910946-10-7 (Paperback)

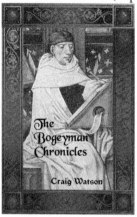

In 14th Century Scotland, amidst the wars of independence, hatred, murder and betrayal are commonplace. People are driven to extraordinary lengths to survive, whilst those with power exercise it with cruel pleasure.

Royal Prince Alexander Stewart, son of King Robert II and plagued by rumours of his illegitimacy, becomes infamous as the Wolf of Badenoch, while young Andrew Christie commits an unforgivable sin and lay Brother Brodie Affleck in the Restenneth Priory pieces together the mystery that links them all together.

From the horror of the times and the changing fortunes of the characters, the legend of the Bogeyman is born and Craig Watson cleverly weaves together the disparate lives of the characters into a compelling historical mystery that will keep you gripped throughout.

Over 80 years the lives of three men are inextricably entwined, and through their hatreds, murders and betrayals the legend of Christie Cleek, the bogeyman, is born.

'The Bogeyman Chronicles haunted our imagination long after we finished it' – iScot Magazine

Mere
Carol Fenlon

ISBN: 978-1-910946-37-4 (Kindle)
ISBN: 978-1-910946-36-7 (Paperback)

"There's something about this place. It's going to destroy us if we don't get away."

Reclaimed from the bed of an ancient mere, drained by their forbears 150 years ago, New Cut Farm is home to the Askin family. Life is hard, but the land and its dark history is theirs, and up till now that has always been enough.

But Con Worrall can't make it pay. Pressured by his new wife following his mother's death, Con reluctantly sells up.

For Lynn Waters, New Cut Farm is the life she has always dreamed of, though her husband Dan has misgivings about the isolated farmhouse.

As Con's life disintegrates and Dan's unease increases, the past that is always there takes over and Lynn discovers the terrible hold that the land exerts over people – and the lengths to which they will go to keep it.

'This a gripping, moving and disturbing read which, like the landscape it describes, takes hold of you and doesn't let go until the last page.'

Over Here
Jane Taylor

ISBN: 978-0-9929768-3-5 (eBook)
ISBN: 978-0-9929768-2-8 (Paperback)

'It's coming up to twenty-four hours since the boy stepped down from the big passenger liner – it must be, he reckons foggily – because morning has come around once more with the awful irrevocability of time destined to lead nowhere in this worrying new situation. His temporary minder on board – last spotted heading for the bar some while before the lumbering process of docking got underway – seems to have vanished for good. Where does that leave him now? All on his own in a new country: that's where it leaves him. He is just nine years old.'

An eloquently written novel tracing the social transformations of a century where possibilities were opened up by two world wars that saw millions of men move around the world to fight, and mass migration to the new worlds of Canada and Australia by tens of thousands of people looking for a better life.

Through the eyes of three generations of women, the tragic story of the nine year old boy on Liverpool docks is brought to life in saddeningly evocative prose.

'...a sweeping haunting first novel that spans four generations and two continents...' – Cristina Odone/Catholic Herald

The Birds That Never Flew
Margot McCuaig

Shortlisted for the Dundee International Book Prize 2012
Longlisted for the Polari First Book Prize 2014
ISBN: 978-0-9929768-4-2 (Paperback)
ISBN: 978-0-9929768-5-9 (ebook)

'Have you got a light hen? I'm totally gaspin.'

Battered and bruised, Elizabeth has taken her daughter and left her abusive husband Patrick. Again. In the bleak and impersonal Glasgow housing office Elizabeth meets the provocatively intriguing drug addict Sadie, who is desperate to get her own life back on track.

The two women forge a fierce and interdependent relationship as they try to rebuild their shattered lives, but despite their bold, and sometimes illegal attempts it seems impossible to escape from the abuse they have always known, and tragedy strikes.

More than a decade later Elizabeth has started to implement her perfect revenge – until a surreal Glaswegian Virgin Mary steps in with imperfect timing and a less than divine attitude to stick a spoke in the wheel of retribution.

Tragic, darkly funny and irreverent, The Birds That Never Flew is a new and vibrant voice in Scottish literature.

'...dark, beautiful and moving...' – scanoir.co.uk

Gemmano
David Will
ISBN: 978-1-910946-42-8 (Paperback)
ISBN: 978-1-910946-43-5 (Kindle)

Northern Italy, 1944: Gemmano is on the front lines of the battle for the Gothic Line, trapped between German occupation and the allied advance, as shell after shell rains down on the village.

Eighteen year old Toni Mazzanti has always been considered 'odd' by the villagers, but as the battle rages and he comes to terms with his personal and spiritual development, his talents come to be viewed as gifts.

With his new found confidence Toni increasingly emerges as a village leader, aided by Lorenzo Bergamas, a young Italian soldier returning from the Front.

Covering a period of ten days, Gemmano is a compelling and inspiring story of people caught powerless in their own land, told from the perspective of two young Italian men.

With empathy and compassion David Will conveys the trauma experienced by the villagers as their homes were destroyed around them, and with a rare intimacy imparts a strong sense of the will to survive that brought them through the carnage of the battle.

Printed in Great Britain
by Amazon